AMALIE

There was a girl gathering flowers in the garden. She wore an ankle-length dress, and her hair—so pale a blond it was almost white—hung longer than her waist, held by a velvet band. She was singing an old English ballad I'd learned in school.

Shadow neighed and snorted and the girl straightened. She was shorter than I, but about my age, I thought with pleasure. Suddenly the idea of a girlfriend, somebody from my own world, on Dorr Island, was enormously appealing.

Then she turned and it was as if a cloud passed across the sun. As I had the night I'd awakened to the presence in my room, I felt cold. And I understood the Gullah use of double adjectives for emphasis. Because this wasn't a girl in front of me at all. And it wasn't a fashionable Laura Ashley dress. The dress, and the woman wearing it, were *old old*.

WHISPER
OF THE
CAT

Norma Johnston

BANTAM BOOKS

TORONTO · NEW YORK · LONDON · SYDNEY · AUCKLAND

RL 6, IL age 12 and up

WHISPER OF THE CAT
A Bantam Book / April 1988

*The Starfire logo is a registered trademark of
Bantam Books.
Registered in U.S. Patent and Trademark Office
and elsewhere.*

ISBN 0-553-26947-X

Published simultaneously in the United States and Canada

*Bantam Books are published by Bantam Books, a division of
Bantam Doubleday Dell Publishing Group, Inc. Its trademark,
consisting of the words ''Bantam Books'' and the portrayal of
a rooster, is Registered in U.S. Patent and Trademark Office
and in other countries. Marca Registrada. Bantam Books, 666
Fifth Avenue, New York, New York 10103.*

PRINTED IN THE UNITED STATES OF AMERICA

O 0 9 8 7 6 5 4 3 2 1

For Cynthia Kane

Author's Note

The speech of Zipporah Bayne and other Dorr Island characters in *Whisper of the Cat* is not "incorrect English." It is Gullah, the language of the islands off the South Carolina and Georgia coasts—a distinct and beautiful language with a consistent, sophisticated grammar of its own.

Gullah is a mixture of West African languages, Caribbean Creole (Carib & Arawak Indian, English, French, Spanish, African), pidgin English (used by West African traders), and English. Its most important quality, however, is its African roots. According to the book and television show, *The Story of English*, Gullah is closer than any other American variety of English to the original Creole English of the New World, and "the lost pidgin English" of the slave ships.

I'm indebted to *The Story of English* by Robert

McCrum, William Cran, and Robert MacNeil, and to *The Lost Legacy of Georgia's Golden Isles* by Betsy Fancher, for information on Gullah language and life. If I've made any mistakes in the wording of Dorr Island dialogue, I trust Gullah-speaking readers will forgive me. The language is so musical and beautiful that I could not write about the sea islands and leave it out.

Chapter One

As the plane dipped its silver wing and swooped low toward the Georgia coastline, I was as nervous as a cat. Not just because I hadn't seen my father for so many years. Not just because I was about to meet a new stepmother for the very first time. There was something else, something I couldn't identify but felt in the marrow of my bones.

"Tracy, stop being silly!" I told myself sternly. But it didn't work. The shiver still was there. I wondered if Mother was feeling the same way herself right now, as she flew on another plane toward a new job, new life, in Buenos Aires.

Maybe my nervousness was natural. After all, there were a lot of things we hadn't talked about before my short-notice trip to Bonne Espérance this summer. I was thinking of that while the plane dropped lower and lower. The pattern of sunset streaks in the sky reminded me of the weird mixture of elation and apprehension in my stomach and in my heart.

On the surface, my trip to the lovely, eerie lowlands of Dorr Island was very uncomplicated. I was going there because of Mother's unexpected South American job offer.

But it seemed so strange that, after ten years my mother and father were practically exchanging lifestyles. I scarcely knew my father. I'd been six when he left for a "hardship post" overseas, and Mother and I were not allowed to go along. I knew little about his life then. I still didn't know much, except that it always seemed terribly glamorous and till now involved some kind of government work.

There were three years of occasional visits—in Paris or in Wisconsin, where Mother and I had lived on her father's farm. I had vague memories of Dad, tall and tanned, bringing me presents that were sometimes wildly improbable. And the time he took me to see *Sleeping Beauty* in Chicago. I was wild about ballet when I was eight, and I still loved it, though I'd long since faced the fact I'd never be a ballerina. Actually, I didn't know *what* I wanted to be.

Mother was different. Mother had been a housewife. When I was ten, she decided to go back to college to finish the studies she'd dropped when she got married. When I was thirteen, I stayed home with Grandpa while my parents had a month's European holiday to celebrate Mom's getting her B.S. degree. Something must have happened—I don't know what—because Mom came home and announced she and Dad had decided on a friendly divorce. They'd grown apart. She'd become interested in a career in the oil industry, of all things, and enrolled in a graduate program. I didn't know what *Dad* had become interested in, because where he was stationed in Africa was too dangerous for me to visit.

Now I was sixteen. A year ago Grandpa died, and

Mother got her master's degree and an oil company job, and Dad remarried. Now Mother was becoming the nomad, and Dad, who'd always said he'd been born a rolling stone, was settling down. I got the letter telling me about it the same May afternoon that Mother came home bursting with the news of her Argentine transfer.

> . . . *sorry it's taken me so long to let you know we're back in the States for good, but when I took my twenty-year retirement from government work in January, I wasn't sure what our plans would be. Then Catriona found out she'd inherited this plantation on one of the Sea Islands of Georgia. She's inherited the whole island actually. Dorr Island's been in her family since the eighteenth century.*
>
> *Catriona has fond memories of vacationing there as a child. It's her dream place really. She's an archaeologist, you know* (I didn't, or at least had not remembered), *so even aside from family sentiment the place has a fascination for her. And now that your father has a contract to write a book—pause for drumroll and loud cheers, please, honey!—Bonne Espérance seemed like a perfect place for us to live.*
>
> *I didn't write you about all this sooner because we didn't know when we'd get back to the States, and we couldn't be sure what shape we'd find the place in. Talk about self-fulfilling prophecies! Bonne Espérance hadn't been occupied in years—or at least it wasn't supposed to have been!—so you can imagine how things ran down, especially in this climate. But over the past three months we've made the place habitable at least,*

*though it's still a bit primitive. So if there's a
chance of your paying us a visit some time this
summer, we'd both love to have you. . . .*

Mother had to relocate in Argentina just as soon
as I finished my junior year in high school. I wanted
to stay with friends in Wisconsin for my senior year,
but she wasn't thrilled with my plan. And no way did
the idea of Argentina thrill me as much as it did her.
Without saying anything, I wrote my father asking if,
just maybe, I could go down there as soon as school
was out, and live with him and Catriona during my
senior year. Two days later I received a telegram:

DEAR TRACY,
    YES YES YES.
      LOVE,
      DAD.

To my astonished joy Mother agreed it was a
sensible idea. So there I was, at the end of June, about
to step off the airplane into a whole new life.

The sunset colors were already fading outside the
airport's plate-glass windows as I hurried toward the
luggage carousel where Dad had said he'd meet me.

Dad wasn't there. For an instant panic seized me.
Then a hand touched my shoulder and a husky alto
voice said, "Tracy? It *is* you, isn't it?"

I spun around.

It had to be Catriona, although I noticed her voice
didn't have a trace of a southern accent. I knew even
before her eyes widened with a look of startled pleasure. "I'd know you now, even if I hadn't seen pictures
of you! You look so much like Kenneth! The same

chin and cheekbones, and the same dark auburn hair. That didn't show up in the photographs."

"They're three years old. My hair's gotten darker since then," I said dazedly. I was startled too. First because Catriona was so much younger than I'd expected. Maybe in her late twenties, but no more. Second because, in spite of the crisp dark linen suit and the up-to-the-minute cut of her pale blond hair, there was something about Catriona—something very old and warm and quiet. I could hardly believe we were meeting for the very first time.

I felt myself smiling, and Catriona smiled, too, with pure relief. "Your green eyes light up the same way your father's do." She took a deep breath. "Thank heaven that's over! I've been mentally rehearsing what we'd say to each other all the way in from Bonne Espérance. Your father had to fly up to New York unexpectedly yesterday, and left me to introduce myself. . . . You can't imagine how nervous I've been."

"Tell me about it," I said ruefully. My large suitcase came jiggling toward us on the carousel, and I grabbed it. Catriona grabbed the other. "What did Dad go to New York for? His book?" I asked as we pushed the luggage cart toward the exit.

"Something like that," Catriona said vaguely. "Look, Tracy, suppose you take care of the luggage while I run and hail a cab." Without waiting for my answer, she was off, her high heels flashing.

She had a cab waiting at the curb when I reached it, and we tumbled in. "To the docks, quickly," she ordered crisply. "I promised Mark we'd be back to the island before dark," she added for my benefit, "and we're pushing it."

Who was Mark? I wondered, but I didn't ask.

Everything—expectations, apprehensions, the move, the trip itself—was piling up on me. I sat back, bemused, looking out the window at a strange new world.

Pine trees and Spanish moss—that was what I was most conscious of. I'd seen pictures of Spanish moss, but I hadn't imagined the ghostliness of it, the grayness, the way it swayed in an invisible breeze even though the air was so heavy and still. Heat closed us in, and so did the towering pines. Then we were in Savannah, threading our way through a maze of flowering squares. Lamplight shone through the dusk from the windows of gracious red-brick houses. I felt as if I'd stepped back through time.

We came out by the shore, and the tempo changed. Catriona saw my face and laughed. "This is our tourist and disco territory. Actually, it was the red-light district in the bad old days. Mark will probably show it to you, if you like." She broke off, because the taxi was coming to a stop.

While Catriona paid the driver I stepped out onto a weathered dock. Sail-, speed-, and fishing boats bobbed gently. A shaft of moonlight cut through the twilight, picking out the silvery lines of a sleek speedboat. Its prow thrust arrogantly forward; its cabin and jutting fins looked like they were made completely of black Plexiglas. A chrome antenna soared as though it were some futuristic moonship. The lettering on its side was French—*Le Chat d'Argent. The Silver Cat.*

There was something catlike, and equally arrogant, about the young man standing in the stern. His feet were bare, his white pants in startling contrast to his black T-shirt, his arms folded across his chest in obvious impatience. His hair was black, too, and his eyes. He turned them on me, slowly, insolently.

A hot flush ran through me. Then, deliberately,

he turned away from me and toward Catriona. The red spell broke, and was succeeded by something like a chill.

Something in my bones was saying this was no casual meeting. I knew uneasily that this boy—no, this *man*—could read me like a book if he chose to. Right now he didn't choose to. But one day he might.

Chapter Two

"You're late," he said flatly.

"I know it," Catriona answered coolly. Then beneath her poise a flash of anger stirred. "The *Silver Cat* belongs to Bonne Espérance, remember? It's all right for you to use her when we don't need her—so long as you're available to skipper her when we need you to. And so long as we know about it."

For a minute their eyes locked, and sparks almost flared. Then he snapped to attention with a formal salute. "Aye, aye, ma'am."

Catriona, after a moment, laughed. "Oh, Mark, snap out of it. And say hello to Tracy Fairbrother. Tracy, this is my cousin Mark Dulaine."

Her cousin . . . that explained a lot. Or did it? It certainly didn't explain the anger I felt when he pointedly ignored me. Or the electricity that tingled through me when he held my hand to steady me as I climbed aboard.

Catriona sat down in the outdoor seating area. I sat down beside her. Mark cast off. The *Silver Cat* leaped through the water, leaving the lights and music of waterfront Savannah far behind. The ride to Dorr Island took almost an hour, and more than once I caught Mark turning to glance at me with an odd expression in his eyes.

After the second time, deliberately, I went to stand behind his pilot's seat, holding tight to the dark Plexiglas shield to keep my balance.

"*Le Chat d'Argent*. Why a French name? And why the *Silver Cat*?"

Mark didn't answer. After a minute, uncomfortable, I turned back to my seat.

Soon after that I became aware of Catriona watching me with troubled eyes. I turned to her impulsively. "Catriona, what—"

My question was never finished. The *Silver Cat* made an abrupt turn, and as it did so the moon suddenly broke through clouds.

Dorr Island loomed before us, like something out of a dark fairy tale, all shrouded and silent. Beyond the white sand beach a forest of pines guarded it, enormously tall, enormously old, and bearded thick with moss. Between beach and forest the marshes stretched, wild and lonely, the sea grasses swaying and whispering of immemorial secrets.

I found myself staring at Catriona. Catriona returned a faint, enigmatic smile.

All at once I had the feeling that something was walking over my grave. I wished suddenly and fervently that my father were with us. Then Mark spun the boat again, abruptly, into an inlet, and my heart stilled.

We were approaching a small, shabby dock, and from it a wide drive swept between a line of trees to a plantation mansion. That was the only word for it. Bonne Espérance loomed foursquare, its pink stucco turned to silver by the moonlight, its white-painted wrought-iron galleries like silver lace. At the dock a gray horse waited patiently between wagon shafts. Mark killed the motor, tied up at the dock, and sprang out to heave my luggage on the wagon. He looked at Catriona. "Want me to drive you up?" he asked grudgingly.

"Thanks, we'll manage," Catriona said. "You go ahead. You're not going far, are you?"

"Over to St. Simons with Cuffy for a jam session." *If it's any of your business,* his tone implied. As if thinking better of it, he added brusquely, "I won't be late."

"Good. I'd like to get an early start tomorrow," Catriona said briskly. "Mark's helping me with my dig," she explained as we drove toward the plantation house.

"Your . . . dig?"

Catriona giggled, seeming suddenly much younger. "Didn't your father tell you I'm an archaeologist? It took graduate school, and the work I was doing in Paris, to make me realize what a historical treasure trove might be right here, where I used to rummage around as a child. When I think of the damage Bini and I must have done, playing with artifacts we found while digging in the sand." She shook her head. "Bonne Espérance was founded by my Dulaine ancestors. They were French, which answers the question you asked earlier about *Le Chat d'Argent.* Old Pierre Dulaine had a land grant from Louis the Fourteenth. Probably for reprehensible services rendered. It was during the French Revolution that the family really settled in here, those who managed to escape the Terror."

The gray horse stopped of his own accord. I looked up, and something tightened in my throat. Up close, Bonne Espérance was like a young girl imprisoned inside the body of an old, old woman. The white paint was peeling on the two matching flights of steps that swirled toward each other up to the main double doors, a full story above the ground. Lights glowed through floor-length windows, and through the fanlight above the door a crystal chandelier glittered.

Carrying one suitcase as she took the other, I followed my new stepmother up the stairs. The double doors opened as we approached, and we walked into splendor.

There was a huge central hall, with scenic wallpaper in blue and green showing scenes of an old seaport, above white paneling. There were elaborately carved white door frames, with mahogany doors opening into a pale gold dining room on the left and a cedar-paneled library on the right. There was a threadbare Persian rug, and a round center table with a brass statue on it, a half-dressed woman holding an elaborate candelabra. High above me the great chandelier winked like a thousand eyes, and another double flight of stairs wound up to darkness.

Catriona touched my shoulder. "Tracy? You look ready to keel over. Would you rather go to your room and rest before dinner, or eat right now and then go up for good?"

"Eat," I said thickly.

I can't tell you what we ate that night, except that it was some kind of seafood stew, spicy and good. There was just the two of us at the long table, with a pleasant elderly black woman serving us. Her name was Zipporah, and she had known Catriona since she was a baby. "You put that child to bed right now, and leave her be," she told Catriona firmly when I started falling asleep over my pecan pie.

Before I knew it, I was upstairs in the right front bedroom, being tucked by Catriona into an enormous canopied bed. "My room's in the back left corner. I'm going to watch TV for a while in the sitting room next to it. If you wake up in an hour or so, come in and join me," Catriona said. I think I was asleep before she left the room.

The next thing I knew, it was the middle of the night, and I was sitting bolt upright in bed, and my heart was hammering. I could not move. *Something* was in the room.

I said *something*, not *someone*, because I could see nothing. Nothing but the looming, motionless shapes of the bedposts, the gilt-trimmed chest, and the armoire. Nothing but them were reflected in the standing mirror. The two floor-length French windows, one on the front and one on the side of the house, both stood ajar, and moonlight flooded in, illumining things clearly.

There was no one but me in the room, and still I felt a presence.

Outside the windows the marsh grasses sighed, and there was a hum of insects. Then, distantly, there was the sound of a boat horn, and that broke the spell. I was able to move my hand and put on the bedside lamp. The light showed nothing I had not already seen. I slid out of bed and walked to the side window.

It opened, as apparently did all the windows, onto the encircling gallery. I stepped out and looked. In the shrubbery below, on the spread of lawn between the house and the surrounding forest, nothing moved. I looked in the direction of Catriona's sitting room. No lights showed. It must be very late.

The boat horn came again, closer now. I moved around to the front of the house and looked down the drive toward the dock. Faintly I could see a moving streak of silver. Mark and the *Silver Cat*, returning? If so, he'd stayed out a lot later than he'd led Catriona to expect.

But that was none of my business. I didn't care what he did, I told myself sternly. By now I was wide enough awake that the fear that had wakened me had vanished. I was glad Mark would never know about it. I felt silly enough as it was. Because clearly there was not and never had been anyone or anything in my room.

I went in through the front window. My legs felt a little weak with relief, so I sat down on the small love seat with its worn covering of pink and blue French brocade.

My fingers stroked the ribbon pattern absently. And froze. A chill ran down my spine, and the hair on my neck seemed to stand straight up. *My hackles rose.* . . . I never believed in that expression before, but I did now. Because the satin brocade my fingers stroked was *warm*. As though someone or something had been sitting there, invisible, for some time.

Chapter Three

Sunlight flooding through the open windows woke me the next morning. A faint breeze, like a kitten's paw, brushed playfully across my face. I lay in bed, taking in the satin-striped white wallpaper with its faded forget-me-not garlands, the heavy nineteenth-century mahogany furniture with its shabby but pretty brocades, pale pinks, and blues. The full-length pier-glass mirror standing across the corner reflected the sheer white curtains and bed hangings, stirring slightly in the breeze.

That must have been what I'd become aware of last night. All at once I felt very sheepish, remembering my conviction of a ghostly presence. And also, suddenly, I was very hungry. I hadn't eaten much at dinner, the hands of the clock on the little gilt-trimmed chest stood at eight, and a tantalizing smell of cinnamon and strong coffee was drifting up to me.

I jumped out of bed and in and out of the next-door bathtub. There wasn't any shower, but the tub, raised up on lion's feet, was long enough to lie down in, and the old-fashioned washbowl had a gray marble counter. By a quarter past eight, in jeans and my favorite bright green top, I was running down the swirling stairs.

"Tracy! Good morning!" Catriona, at one end of the dining room's long table, looked up, smiling, as I slid into my chair. "I'm glad you got down while Zipporah's cinnamon buns are still fresh. She's famous for them in the Sea Islands, aren't you, Zipporah?"

Zipporah, who had been hovering, just waved the compliment away, but her dark eyes held a gleam of satisfaction.

"I'm sorry I'm late for breakfast," I mumbled, sinking my teeth into one of the heavenly confections.

"Don't be. I let you sleep on purpose. You must have been exhausted—you were out like a light when I looked in on you fifteen minutes after we went upstairs. Zipporah, pass Tracy the scrambled eggs and grits, will you, please? *I* eat early because I'm a working woman, but this is your summer vacation, so you sleep as late as you want," Catriona went on. "Did you sleep straight through?"

Was I imagining things, or was there a trace of anxiety beneath her brisk cheerfulness? "I'd better be a working woman, too, as soon as I can find a summer job." I helped myself to eggs and the unfamiliar-looking white hominy Zipporah held out to me in a silver casserole. My heart began to hammer slightly. "No, I didn't sleep through. I had the weirdest—dream, I guess it was. All of a sudden, in the middle of the night, I was wide-awake. I could have sworn someone was in the room with me. But there was no one there."

This time there was no mistaking it. The room, and everything in it, seemed to become alert. The silver casserole lid in Zipporah's hands clattered against its base.

"*Chat d'Argent,*" she muttered beneath her breath.

"Zipporah, these eggs are cold. Be an angel and get us some hot ones," Catriona interrupted sharply. When the housekeeper had left, she relaxed again. "You're not serious about a job, are you? Ken and I certainly didn't expect you to earn your keep, if that's what you're thinking."

I shook my head firmly. "If I were back in Wisconsin, I'd be working in a fast-food place or something. Everybody does. I'll be going to college in another year, and, well . . ." I finished lamely. It had already dawned on me that despite the grandeur of silver, gilt, and crystal, Bonne Espérance was not merely shabby, it was practically falling apart. Now it was sinking in on me that there weren't likely to be any supermarkets or fast-food places in need of temporary help on Dorr Island. I'd have to go to the mainland, and it was pretty clear that wasn't easy.

Zipporah came back in, bringing a fresh batch of cinnamon buns and eggs. Her face was impassive. When she'd left again, Catriona looked at me directly. "Look, Tracy, it's your dad's place to be talking finances with you, but heaven knows when he's getting back—"

I did a double take, and she broke off and grinned. "He phoned late last night. Problem with the publisher—he has to go to Washington to make sure he has clearance to write about certain things. I hope he gets it," she added as I blinked.

A new set of question marks were beginning to bristle in my mind. I put them aside as Catriona went on. "As I was saying, since he's not here, I guess I should start acting like a stepmother and relieve your mind. Ken *expects* to pay for your education. Your mother wants to be a part of it too—I know they talked

on the phone about it before she left." That was an
eye-opener for me. "Both of them are doing pretty
well now, you know. Your mother has a great job,
and Ken has his government pension. Not to mention
a whacking big advance on his book. Nobody's rolling
in wealth, but you don't have to worry about college,
or food on your plate, or a roof over your head. Even
if it does leak."

Catriona glanced pointedly at the rust spots on
the sculptured ceiling, and I giggled.

"I did notice," I confessed.

"How could you help it?" Catriona laughed.
"The first day we walked through this place, your
father told me only Dulaine pride and pigheadedness
kept it standing! We made sure the worst hazards to
life and limb were taken care of before we let you
come here, and I'm working on the rest of the resto-
ration piece by piece. The kitchen, and our bedroom
and sitting room were first on the list. I haven't gotten
to the bathrooms yet, but at least you have a new
mattress and pillows and comforter for your bed. Maybe
by fall I can offer you a bathtub with no rust marks."

"It seems a shame to junk that antique," I said.
"If Dad's book contract is so great . . . it doesn't seem
fair that just because Dad's stuck with me and my
education—"

Catriona shook her head. "Bonne Espérance is
Dulaine territory, and it's going to be Dulaine income
that will fix it up. Dorr Island's my baby, and I support
it. And if that's pigheaded, I guess you and Ken are
just stuck with it. Bonne Espérance is my project, just
the way his book is your father's, and college is yours.
What are you going to major in, do you know?"

"I'm not sure. I was thinking history, but last
winter I took a course in sociology. I want to know

what makes people what they are." I took a deep breath and shook my head. "It's funny, I was thinking yesterday on the plane—it's not just you and I who don't know each other. I've no idea what Dad's life's been like, or what he does, or even what his book's about."

"It's about his experiences in overseas trouble spots, and how cultural differences between different peoples can cause misunderstandings that can escalate into major crises. It's probably going to ruffle a lot of official feathers, because your father thinks ethnocentrism is a major American weakness." Catriona chuckled. "It sounds to me like you and your father have a lot in common."

"Like you two do?"

"You picked up on that, did you?" Catriona said with respect. She finished her cup of coffee and stood suddenly. "Let me show you the house before I get to work. We'll start up under the leaky roof and work our way down."

I followed her up yet another flight of curving stairs.

The uppermost hall was square and bright with sunlight flooding in through the ceiling dome of leaded glass. From a great brass loop at its center, a frayed and faded rope of dark blue velvet supported the chandelier that dangled far below.

"Don't worry, there's a heavy chain inside the velvet sleeve," Catriona said, noting my alarm. "The chain's sturdy, and replacing the velvet's not at the top of my priority list since we're not planning any grand balls in the near future. Maybe we'll have a party here when your father's book comes out."

She opened heavy mahogany double doors, and I gasped aloud.

I'd never seen a ballroom, but I knew immediately

that was what this was. It ran across the entire front of the house. The dark floor, even with a thin layer of dust upon it, gleamed. Gilt metal cornices, elaborate above blue velvet draperies, gleamed too. *Three* crystal chandeliers caught the sunlight and sent it in rainbow fragments to bounce off matching crystal-and-gilt wall brackets and gilt-framed mirrors. A small army of little ebony-and-gilt chairs backed up against white paneling. Their seats, and the walls above the paneling, were the same soft blue brocade that was in the hall.

"Old St. Pierre used to hold swinging parties up here in his day," Catriona said, amused at my dazed reaction.

"St. Pierre?"

"I'll tell you about him when we get downstairs." Catriona herded me back into the hall, shutting the doors behind us. A number of other doors rimmed the hall, but she made no move toward them. "This floor's mostly attics and storage, so we keep it locked. I don't want squirrels or other prowlers getting in! Mark sleeps in that corner room on the right, and he's probably got that locked up too."

There was a cryptic note in Catriona's voice. I looked at her impulsively as we went downstairs. "He's your cousin? Are you close?"

"Actually his father was my first cousin. And 'close' depends on in what sense you mean," Catriona said frankly. "I used to spend summers here when I was little, and he was a baby who was brought here for visits once or twice. That must have been eighteen years ago. His parents died when he was around ten, and he was sent to live with his grandparents, and then *he* spent summers here. Sometime in his teens he had a huge fight with them and was sent away to school.

He still hasn't told me what the fight was about! My parents died in an accident when I was in college, and then his grandfather died."

"Is that how you inherited Bonne Espérance?" I asked.

Catriona nodded. "I was the only child of an eldest son. After my parents died, Mark's grandparents used to spend summers here—to his grandmother's great disgust." Catriona's lip curled. "She preferred Palm Beach or Beverly Hills, and she took off for one or the other as soon as her husband died. I hadn't seen Mark for years and years—till Ken and I arrived here this winter."

"You don't mean he just walked in on you and stayed?" I asked incredulously. Then I reddened. That was pretty close to what I'd done myself.

"Walked in on us, nothing. He was already here. He'd finished school last June and headed straight here, without a word to his grandmother. He set up housekeeping in that room he'd had as a child, and nearly scared the wits out of both of us when he loomed like a ghost out of the shadows. Don't look like that, Tracy; he didn't *break* in. There'd been vagrants here before, and there were windows broken. Mark had boarded them up, and fixed up that room, and gotten the old kerosene stove working. He'd rehabilitated a boat—"

"Not the *Silver Cat!*"

"Oh, no. Ken bought that for us after Mark's old wooden hulk blew up in an accident. Fortunately," Catriona said soberly, "he wasn't on it. He'd remembered a textbook he'd forgotten and run back toward the house only minutes before. The boat was totally destroyed, and the dock nearly."

"Textbook?" I parroted dumbly. The picture Catriona had painted was all too vivid before my eyes.

"Mark had enrolled in college in Savannah. He was paying his way fishing, and taking fishing and sight-seeing parties around the islands."

So Catriona let him stay. It made me warm to her all the more.

We were on the second floor, which was really the main floor, now. Here the wallpaper above the low white paneling was acid-green stripes with a thin blue border, on a white ground. "The drawing room," Catriona said, opening doors. "Grandmamma would have killed me if I called it a living room."

I could see why. It was directly above the dining room. Its fireplace was black marble. Against a background of pale green, the furniture was opulent Victorian, heavily carved and tufted. Everything was peacock-blue, or royal, or emerald. Everything, except the white gauze curtains with their bead-fringed borders, was silk brocade. It might be worn through, or water-stained, or faded, but it reeked of bygone grandeur.

From a heavy gold frame above the mantel the painted face of an arrogant man in a black velvet suit seemed to gaze at us. His blue-black hair was tied at the nape of his neck with a satin bow, one hand gripped a sword-hilt, and the dark eyes were almost frighteningly alive.

That was not why I shivered. It was because the face, the bearing, above all those eyes in which violence was thinly veiled, were like a mirror image of Mark Dulaine.

Chapter Four

"Looks alarmingly like Mark, doesn't he?" Catriona had come silently up behind me.

"Catriona, who is he?" I asked dazedly.

Instead of answering, she opened a hidden door in the paneling at one end of the room. "This is your father's and my private suite, if you'll excuse my grandeur." It ran across the rear of the house. First the long bedroom, furnished much like mine but cheerful with a modern print of peach, apricot, and pale blue. A tiny bath had been squeezed in as Catriona said, and beyond it was a small sitting room, beige and cocoa, newly furnished with comfortable sofa, chairs, and hassocks. There was a corner fireplace like in my room; there was a large TV and stereo. A sweater in progress lay on one of the swivel rockers; the jacket of one of my favorite records was on top of the stereo. It was very cheerful, very lived-in, very different from the rest of Bonne Espérance with its sense of being shrouded in ghosts of the past.

22

"This feels like home," I heard myself saying, and Catriona turned to me with a sudden warm smile.

"I'm very glad."

From the rear gallery outside the master suite, spiral iron stairs ran down to the gallery below and also up, to disappear into the ceiling. "They go through a trap door into the storage room," Catriona said. "There are stairs from the gallery below down to what at any normal house would be the backyard. Let's go down the outside way. After the third floor I can use some fresh air."

We picked our way down the spiral steps. "That's the kitchen and pantry, behind the dining room," Catriona said, pointing. "Let's not bother Zipporah, she's not feeling well." She turned in through open French doors. "This is where I work, for the moment. When your father gets to the writing stage of his book, he'll probably take this over. By then I'll have outgrown this room, and will have to rehabilitate the ground-level space for a museum."

"For a *what?*"

"That's what this is all going to turn into probably. A living-history museum of a . . . unique aspect of American southern life." Catriona smiled a bit crookedly. "I started out to dig into the legends of my own family, and thanks to my scientific training, I unlocked a Pandora's box."

"What did you find out?" I asked, fascinated.

She hesitated. "It's a long story! Let's sit down, Tracy, and I'll tell you all about Bonne Espérance and the long shadow of St. Pierre. And if you're interested, I can offer you that summer job you want."

I sat down, already certain that I'd be interested in both the history of the plantation and the job, whatever it was. Catriona sat down, too, on the other side of the long table she was using as a desk. The room was sunny and cheerful, cedar-paneled: a shabby, homey place where real work was done. But as she talked, it was as though invisible shadows lengthened over the room.

"I'm ashamed to say that Bonne Espérance, like other plantations in the Deep South, represents splendor built on the blood and sweat of a slave economy. The original Paul Dulaine received Dorr Island as a land grant from one of the Louis. Probably for unspecified services, after which the king preferred to have him far away! He brought in the slaves and started the first rice fields, and built the cellars and first two levels of the manor house.

"He died in a duel, and his son Pierre inherited." Catriona glanced at me. "That was his portrait you saw upstairs. Whatever his father might have been and done, Pierre was and did more—and worse. I won't go into details now, but let's just say that the worst excesses TV and rock videos dream up in the way of decadence were matched by Pierre Dulaine. Sex, drugs, sadism—you name it. He *owned* Dorr Island, so he was judge and jury, and there was no court of appeals. That's why he was called *St.* Pierre—St. Peter—but only behind his back. Because he could send you to heaven or to hell."

"You're kidding!"

"I'm afraid not. He was brutal with women, and with slaves. According to legend there was one young slave who was very beautiful. Pierre wanted her. She was in love with another slave, and she fought Pierre off. He killed the man she loved, and then he had her whipped to death with the cat-o'-nine-tails. The natives swear she put a curse on him with her dying breath, and three days later Pierre was found dead in the garden. There wasn't a mark on him except a few cat scratches, and no clue to his death except for the look of inexpressible horror on his face."

"Go on. Which one of them haunts the place?" I asked, only half joking.

"Tracy!" Catriona burst out laughing. "Don't *you* start! It's bad enough listening to Zipporah on the subject. What I need from you is some scientific detachment!"

"I can't promise that. But I want the job. What do I do?"

"Whatever needs doing. I need a notetaker, filekeeper, and gofer. Do you have a driver's license?" Catriona asked, and I nodded. "Good! I keep a car parked over in Savannah, and often I need errands run. Mark will run you to the mainland on the *Silver Cat*. He's helping me with the digs, but because of his fishing and charters, I can't rely on him." She didn't explain what she meant by that. "Basically I'm doing three things. Compiling a family history and cataloging the family papers and other records. Trying to preserve and build up documentation of the social history of a Sea Island slave plantation. And doing a proper archaeological dig on the sites where family records indicate the plantation's life and work took place."

Catriona took a deep breath and grinned. "There! And of course, most unscientifically, I'm trying to do all three things at once! Still want a job?"

"Yes!" We shook hands, formally. "What can I start doing?"

"Suppose you begin by putting all these files on my desk back where they belong?" Catriona pointed to a brown metal file cabinet near the bookcases. "That

will familiarize you with the project. And let's have
some lemonade to celebrate your hiring." She picked
up the telephone and, to my surprise, pushed buttons.
"Intercom. I couldn't see any point in staying histor-
ically accurate and having Zipporah tramping around
on her aching legs answering bells. Not that Zipporah
approves, of course. . . . Zipporah?"

Her voice changed. "Zipporah, if you feel that
poorly, go to bed! This afternoon, like it or not, I'm
taking you to the mainland to a doctor. . . . Zipporah
Bayne, *shut up!* And stay put! I'm not going to argue
the subject on the phone."

Catriona banged the phone down and strode toward the door. "Migraine," she tossed back over her
shoulder. "Zipporah believes in home remedies, not
modern medicine. *And* the circulation in her legs is
so bad, she's really got to have something done about
it. You go ahead and tackle the files. Poke around in
anything you want to. I'll be back as soon as I can."
She vanished.

With her exit something alive and vital seemed
to leave the room. Maybe that was just because I
was alone with my memory of the vivid tale she'd spun
. . . with my memory of last night, and the feeling
that there was something in my room.

I was determined not to give in to my imagination. What was it Catriona had said was needed? Scientific detachment. I could certainly do with some of
that right now. My hands were steady as I filed the
folders in their proper drawers: *Slavery: Auctions* . . .
Emancipation . . . *Reconstruction* . . . *Religion* . . .
Dulaine Family: Correspondence . . . *Personal Profiles*
. . .*Factual Records* . . . *Legends* . . . *Bonne Espérance:
Architectural Plans* . . . *Inventories* . . . *Life-styles* . . .

*Dorr Island: History . . . Economy . . . Genealogies
. . . Language . . . Superstitions . . .*

It was when I was putting away the file marked
Dorr Island Superstitions: Love Charms that I saw it.
Dorr Island Superstitions: Ghosts.

All at once my fingers were less steady. But I
pulled the folder out. I'm not sure what I was looking
for—something about a sense of presence in a midnight
room, or something about Bonne Espérance being
haunted by St. Pierre or the woman he had killed.
What first met my eyes was nothing so spectacular. It
was a piece of yellow legal paper, with a scholarly-
sounding quotation hand-written on it:

> *. . . natives of the Sea Islands, particularly
> of Dorr Island (corruption of Isle d'Or, or Isle of
> Gold) believe, as do many people whose devout
> Christianity is overlaid with generations-old traces
> of the Old Religion (see also Voodoo) that par-
> ticularly sensitive people, deeply good or deeply
> evil, have the power to "send their spirits out,"
> either in disembodied form or in the shape of some
> familiar creature. As the black cat is associated
> with evil spirits, so is the white or silver cat as-
> sociated with beneficent spirits or, in some cases,
> a kind of avenging angel. This beneficent figure
> is often misinterpreted as evil because it brings
> warning of approaching danger.*

A white or silver cat. *Le Chat d'Argent. . . .*

I didn't know why, but at that moment the memory of the portrait of St. Pierre Dulaine rose up before
me. And superimposed upon it, like a moving film
being projected against the old painting, flashed the

image of the *Silver Cat* last night, racing through the sea toward the haunting shadows of Bonne Espérance, with Mark at the wheel. Mark, turning to look at me, his hair gleaming blue-black in the sudden moonlight, his eyes the same as the half-alluring, half-terrifying ones of the St. Pierre portrait.

When Catriona's footsteps creaked on the floor behind me, I almost screamed.

Chapter Five

"Here's the lemonade," Catriona said briskly. "I just spoke to Mark. He'll take you to the mainland for a taste of Savannah nightlife tonight. Tracy? What's the matter?"

"Nothing. You just startled me," I said thickly. I shoved the quotation about silver cats back into its folder, and the folder back into its drawer, and shut that firmly.

Catriona and I spent the rest of the morning working our way companionably through the pileup on her desk, and nothing raised the subject of silver cats, or Mark's resemblance to St. Pierre, or my scare last night.

At one-thirty we broke for lunch, which we foraged for ourselves in the big cool kitchen. Zipporah was still lying down. "She's got ice and a poultice of ground bark on her head," Catriona said when she returned from checking on her. "You'd hardly believe she has a grandson who's a musician and a grand-daughter who's an attorney, would you? She's as pigheaded as the rest of us from Bonne Espérance. With the added touch of Gullah to reinforce it!"

Gullah, I'd learned that morning, was the name given to the lowland blacks and the language and mysterious, spiritual culture they'd brought with them from Africa. Catriona's comment gave me the perfect opening for asking about Dorr Island superstitions— and about Zipporah's muffled exclamation when I spoke about the "presence" in my room. But I didn't take it. I told myself it was because I knew Catriona wouldn't answer me. But that wasn't the whole reason. Even now, while I was sitting across the big kitchen table from Catriona in broad daylight, the remembrance spooked me.

After lunch Catriona suggested a visit to her fieldwork, and we went down the outside steps to the back "yard" that had once been gravel and oyster shells but was now mostly hard-packed dirt. We walked down the crushed-shell path between what Catriona said next year would again be gardens, and then turned off to the left. Forest pressed in close on either side, a strange forest that was part live oak and pine and cedar, and part swamp. Presently we came into a small clearing.

"This *is* a real archaeological dig!" I exclaimed.

Here the forest had been, or was again, held at bay. Here grass grew, and neat rectangles had been staked out like a playing board for some mysterious game. Some of the rectangles had already been dug into. At the far end a little metal toolshed stood, padlocked and secretive.

Some of the rectangles were outlined not just with pegged string but with old stones. Some still had areas of stone floor. No walls still stood, but here and there old stone and masonry chimneys lifted like arms to the bright blue sky. A climbing rosebush, crowded with crimson blooms, flung itself gallantly against one crumbling chimney. Here and there shards of broken pottery poked fingers through the earth. Somewhere, near yet out of sight, the salt marshes sighed with infinite melancholy.

I looked at my stepmother, my eyes brimming, and Catriona looked back at me and read my mind.

"The Bonne Espérance slave quarters," she said quietly. "Strange, isn't it, how peaceful it is here? But the Gullahs have always had a sense that life and death and afterlife are all one. I guess they've had to, to survive. This stone-and-oystershell masonry's called tabby. It's what Bonne Espérance is built of, inside the pink stucco. This is just ordinary pottery. The really precious artifacts are in the cemetery. Gullahs put a person's most loved possessions on her grave, just as has been done for millennia in Africa."

"Like the tombs in Egypt!" I cried. "Come to think of it, that's in Africa too."

"That's right," Catriona said, laughing. "The African kingdoms had some of the most skilled goldworkers the world has ever produced, at a time when Europe was still in the Dark Ages. And St. Pierre Dulaine had the infernal arrogance to call his slaves savage and subhuman! *He*, of all people."

She sat down cross-legged on the earth and began to brush dirt carefully off a graceful sliver of blue pottery. "Blue's supposed to ward off evil spirits. That's why doors, including the doors to the Bonne Espérance cellars, are painted blue."

"What do you do with what you find?" I asked, sitting down too.

"Catalog them on the computer, and try to identify whose and what they were. You can help with that. Then they go down in the cellars, which eventually will turn into a museum."

"The precious things from the cemetery too?"

Catriona shook her head. "I may be a professional archaeologist, but I wouldn't have the effrontery to violate a graveyard. Especially a Gullah graveyard." She finished her excavation of the pottery shard, and set it on her knee. "This is from a rice bowl, I imagine. Getting it out with just fingers was pure luck. It usually requires tools, and delicate hands, and a lot of praying."

I asked her what tools.

"Oh, the whole Hollywood setup—sieves for sifting the dirt, clay modeling tools to dig with, and camel-hair brushes. It's long, hot, painstaking work, and we have to be very careful."

" 'We'?"

Catriona grimaced. "Mark's supposed to be giving me three hours work a day in exchange for room and board. But he has so many irons in the fire, and heaven only knows what they all are or whom he's hanging out with—" She broke off. "But don't worry! If I didn't know you'd be absolutely safe with him tonight, I'd never let you go. Mark will look out for you. I just wonder how much he looks after himself these days."

She looked so perturbed that I changed the subject instead of pursuing it as I'd have liked to. "Catriona, what started you on all this anyway?" I made a comprehensive gesture with my arm.

"I'm not sure. Maybe it was pulling an all-nighter to read *Gone with the Wind* in one sitting when I was eleven. And then seeing the movie. I guess by now it must be thirty times, and the mixture of beauty and brutality never fails to move me. Maybe it's just because I'm a Dulaine, and Dorr Island's in my blood and bone, and it's here, and I'm here. Zipporah's granddaughter Bini and I used to play house out here together when we were six. Now I'm an archaeologist, I live here, and she's a lawyer and wants to take some of her vacation time to come back and help me excavate." She sighed. "I wish all Zipporah's grandchildren were so successful. Bini's cousin Cuffy's probably going to land himself—and Mark—in jail if we don't all look out."

I started to ask what she meant. Distantly, a bell clanged. Catriona scrambled to her feet as if glad for the interruption. "That's at the house. There must be a phone call. Or else Zipporah's worse, in which case I may have to hog-tie her and drag her to a doctor. Want to come along to Savannah for the boat ride?"

"I'll be getting one tonight. I think I'll stay out here and explore."

"*No, you won't.*" Catriona took hold of my shoulders and spun me around to face her. Her sudden gesture took me completely by surprise, and I was shocked by the passion in her voice. "Tracy, listen to me. I'm not trying to alarm you. But you must never go exploring on your own. Not ever. *Never* go out of the big-house clearing until Mark or I have shown you which paths are safe. *Never* go off the paths unless one of us is with you. Never go in the water, by boat or swimming, if you're alone. There are poisonous snakes, and there's quicksand. The marshes aren't safe, and many people have found that navigating through the Sea Islands is the equivalent of negotiating the Bermuda Triangle."

My face must have gone white. Catriona leaned forward and linked her arm through mine. "I'm not trying to spook you. I'm just telling you to take sensible precautions. Now come back to the house and let's gang up together on Zipporah."

I followed her to the house, my mind still spinning with Catriona's warnings. The bell had signaled a telephone call for her. After it was over, we paid a visit to Zipporah's ground-level room, and Zipporah's migraine was bad enough to weaken her fighting spirit. Catriona sent me up to bang on Mark's door and find out whether he wanted to ferry Catriona and Zipporah to the mainland, or have Catriona take the *Silver Cat* herself.

Mark didn't answer. I ran back down to report that he apparently was out, and Zipporah and Catriona glanced at each other. Catriona went to harness up the gray horse, whose name was Shadow, and we helped Zipporah to the wagon, and then to the boat. The elderly woman's legs were very bad. "Blood pressure and circulation," Catriona muttered to me. "Sure you won't come along?"

"Not unless you need me." After Catriona aimed the *Silver Cat* toward the mainland, I tied Shadow to the quay to wait for her return and walked back to Bonne Espérance. I was actually looking forward to having the old house to myself—so long as it was daylight, I added mentally.

I made myself a glass of iced tea, took it to my room, and unpacked. And it was strange; as I laid my tops and jewelry and underclothes in the antique bombé chest, and hung my pants and dresses in the big armoire—eighteenth-century plantation houses apparently did not have closets—I began to feel, more and more strongly, that I had come home.

I wished my father were there.

I stood a framed snapshot of him on one end of

the chest, and my mother's picture on the other. I wondered how my mother was making out in Buenos Aires, and if anyone interesting was showing her around. It would be nice if she found someone, as my father had.

At that moment, and totally without my own volition, Mark's image flashed before me. The realization shook me. Clearly, I was a lot more vulnerable to the St. Pierre kind of guy than I'd known I could be!

He wasn't my type—if I *had* a type, that is. I'd gone out with guys in Wisconsin, nobody serious, but I tended to go for guys who were into sports and school activities. Mark seemed as far from those guys as anyone could get. And yet . . .

I decided I'd better do something active, fast, to distract my mind. Catriona hadn't said anything about not exploring the house, other than staying away from the cellars till she'd shown me through them. So I went downstairs and explored the library with its bays of books, its big outdated globe and folios of old maps and prints, its wing chairs and blue velvet sofa, its Persian rug of threadbare blues and greens, and its malachite-green wallpaper and window swags.

In addition to a round worktable there was a huge heavy desk with drawers on both sides. Books and magazines about America's role in the Middle East lay open on it, as though my father had just set them down, and that warmed me.

I went upstairs and explored the next level, too, avoiding the drawing room with the portrait that was too like Mark, and then climbed again to the top floor. In my imagination the ballroom sprang to life, and I could see a girl with auburn hair and green eyes floating like Scarlett O'Hara in the arms of a tall young man with blue-black hair and eyes like bottomless black pools—I slammed *that* intoxicating picture off, too, blushing violently.

Catriona had said the storerooms were locked, but I tried the door handles anyway, without thinking. The doors held.

The door to the room at the back of the house opened. It was small, much like the guest room next to mine but plainer and dingier. I turned away from it in disappointment, and walked past Mark's door quickly, half laughing at myself because I knew he had not come in.

I approached the next room, directly above the guest room, and all at once the hair on my neck began to prickle. A faint thread of music came from beneath the door. But no one was home. . . . Summoning my courage, I knocked faintly on the door, then knocked again. Nothing happened.

I tried the knob, and the door swung slowly inward.

The room had been a nursery in some bygone time. A white wrought-iron cradle swung beneath a half-canopy of rotting lace. Books and discarded toys lay on the daybed against the wall, on once-white bookshelves, on child-size school desks. A thin layer of dust lay like gossamer over everything.

In the center of it all, on a round marble table, a miniature carousel-horse music box was revolving to the heart-tugging melody of "Clair de Lune."

Deep within me something stirred. Was *this* what had wakened me last night, this thread of music before I reached full consciousness? Why would it have been playing in the middle of the night? How could it be playing now? I picked it up carefully.

All at once the sense of presence behind me was

intense. But it was no ghost. Mark's voice struck me like a blow. "What the hell are you doing here?"

I willed myself to stand tall. "Catriona said I could explore," I said coldly.

"She couldn't have meant for you to pry in here. You could break that music box fiddling with it." He snatched it away.

Even then, furious and startled as I was, I could see how carefully his fingers held it. Long fingers, like an artist's or a musician's . . . or like St. Pierre's in the portrait downstairs.

Mark strode out, then stood waiting pointedly for me to follow. He shut the door after us and stood at the top of the stairs watching as I gathered my dignity around me and descended.

I was halfway down when his voice reached me. "Be ready to leave at six-thirty. I'm buying you dinner in Savannah."

"You don't have to. In fact, you don't have to take me to Savannah at all," I said with spirit.

"Don't be ridiculous," Mark said in an altered voice. And went into his room, slamming the door behind him.

He left me wondering whether this Savannah date was his idea, or Catriona's . . . and wondering why I still was going.

Chapter Six

I had no idea what a "taste of Savannah nightlife" meant. I wasn't sure whether I even wanted to go. In fact, I kept telling myself I wouldn't, all the time I was taking a now badly needed bath in the old tub, and putting on the dress Dad had sent me as a gift last Christmas. It came from India, and the rust-and-black–printed gauze was splashed with gold paint. One of the great things about ethnic clothes was the way they fit in anywhere you wanted to wear them. I hung swinging gold hoops from my ears, slid my bare feet into flat gold sandals, and went downstairs, still feeling undecided.

Mark wasn't there.

The malachite clock in the library tinkled a tune at a quarter to seven and at seven, and still he didn't come. By now my feelings were no longer undecided. I stalked across to Catriona in the dining room. "Scratch the trip to Savannah. Is there enough of that salad you're eating for me to have some too?"

Catriona looked alarmed. "Don't give up yet! I'm

38

sure Mark will be here. His unpunctuality drives me crazy, too, but I'm sure he wouldn't—"

"Oh, wouldn't he?" I asked. "After the way he blew up at me—" I stopped abruptly.

"The way he *what*?"

"Nothing." For some reason I did not quite understand, I didn't want Catriona to know about the scene in the nursery or the music box playing by itself. Not yet. "Look," I said hurriedly, "maybe I misunderstood. I'm going to walk down to the dock. If Mark shows up here, tell him."

Catriona frowned. "Are you sure you want to?"

"Absolutely! I need to cool off, and—" I hesitated. "Is there any reason that I shouldn't?"

"You'll be safe enough if you stick to the drive," Catriona said after a moment's pause. "I only meant that it's starting to get dark, and it's a lonely walk."

"There's still a lot of light. And believe me, if your gorgeous cousin"—why on earth had I said *that*?—"doesn't show up while it *is* still light, I'll be back here faster than the *Silver Cat* can travel! And he can forget this so-called date!"

"Hmm," Catriona said inscrutably, her eyes twinkling.

Twilight was gathering, and beneath the cedars and live oaks with their veils of moss, it was already dark. I stuck strictly to the drive, breathing deeply, and I ran. The night breeze from the water felt good against my face.

I don't know when it was that I first began to feel that something ran beside me. It was so queer. But there was no sound except the murmur of night birds and insects, and the sighing of the marshes. And I was not afraid. I stopped, and whatever it was stopped too, and waited. I started again, more slowly, and it came with me. It was almost as if a guardian angel were watching over me.

"I've been reading too many gothic romances," I thought. But in those novels the spirits were always evil. This one was friendly—

Definitely, the spell of Bonne Espérance was getting to me. And it was high time I stopped letting it, before I got thoroughly spooked.

The *Silver Cat* rocked quietly at her mooring, but there was no sign of Mark Dulaine. "Mark?" I called out, but no sound came from the cabin. The twilight was deepening now, and the water sparkled, mysteriously silver. I put one foot on the *Silver Cat*'s side, and she dipped beneath the slight weight.

"*Don't!*" a voice shouted.

I was so startled that I slipped and almost fell. Mark's arms caught me from behind. "I tried to warn you," he scolded. "This fiberglass can be slippery. The best idea's to step right over the side. Or this." Before I knew what he was doing, he scooped me up and deposited me in the cockpit. Then he jumped in beside me, slid into the pilot's seat, and grinned.

"Showing off or trying to make up for being late?" I asked acidly.

"Neither. Trying to make up for lost time because I'm starved. Aren't you?"

"Sure. I was ready to eat at six-thirty, like you said."

"I had some stuff I had to do first," Mark said calmly. He turned the key—it was almost exactly like starting a car, I noticed—and the *Silver Cat* leaped out from the dock.

The electricity I had sensed between us on the ride last night was still there. So was the sense that he was half challenging, half avoiding me. Stop this, I told myself sternly. Getting involved with Mark would be asking for trouble; Catriona had practically told me so.

I settled myself on the padded white seat, smoothed my skirt, and ignoring my own good advice, asked Mark to tell me about his fishing business.

Mark glanced at me and grinned. "Catriona told you about that, huh? What else did she tell you?"

"Only that you went to college in Savannah, and took sight-seeing and fishing-charter parties out."

"It's a living," Mark said, swinging the *Silver Cat's* nose out of the channel and aiming toward the mainland.

"What are you going to do for a living really?"

"Nosy, aren't you?"

"Maybe it's scientific curiosity," I said loftily. "You're part of Dorr Island, aren't you? I'm going to be helping Catriona with her field research." Was I imagining things, or did something in Mark grow alert? "Tell me about your other boat, the one that blew up."

"It wore out, that's all. I'd been holding the motor together with spit and prayer since I was a kid. And it wasn't my 'other boat.' " There was an edge on Mark's voice. "The *Silver Cat* belongs to your dad, as Cat keeps constantly reminding me." I blinked, and he laughed, restored to humor. "Cat. Short for Catriona, get it? It used to drive her crazy when I called her that when I was little. Still does," he added, eyes gleaming.

"Catriona. It's an odd name."

"It's Gaelic or Celtic or something. The Dulaines came from Brittany. Probably explains why old St. Pierre was so weird. It certainly explains why Cat's superstitious. And why she hates that nickname."

"Catriona's not superstitious!"

"Oh, yes, she is," Mark contradicted. "Scratch

that scientific surface and she's pure Celt. And pure Dorr Islander. If it's in your blood, you never get rid of it."

"Oh?" I asked, inviting him to say more.

Mark's answer was to slam on the gas. The *Silver Cat* leaped like a flying fish. The lights of Savannah were ahead of us now, coming ever closer. We swooped up at the dock where I'd first seen Mark the night before. Now, after dark, it was different. People were strolling along the shore walk, and bursts of laughter and music came from the cafés. Lights and neon signs glowed through the mist.

Mark jumped ashore and tied up at the dock. Then he held out a hand to help me out. His mood had changed; he could have been any boy I'd meet back home, taking me on a first date, and I felt reassured. Then, as we began heading off the dock area toward the restaurant he had in mind, something happened.

It really wasn't any one thing. First a small knot of young black men, hanging out beneath a streetlight, separated. One of them came toward us, and I remember noticing that he was good-looking. I remember how the light picked up the purple stripe in his madras shirt, and how it made the purple gleam. He didn't say anything, but he caught Mark's eye, and with a muttered "Excuse me," Mark went to meet him.

They talked for a minute in the shadows cast by the moored boats, and in that minute I felt again that prickling sensation of being watched. Not by them. By someone else, unseen, who was watching Mark and me.

It was only a slight awareness, like a cold breeze suddenly stirring. Then Mark came back. He linked his arm through mine and said, "I'm starved. How about some crab cakes?"

I let him lead me into a restaurant that was small, and lantern-lit, and cheerfully noisy. The crab cakes were very good. After we ate, Mark announced that the only proper way to see Savannah was by horse and carriage, and he summoned one with a flourish in the lamp-lit square.

"This is going to cost an arm and a leg!" I protested.

"Forget it! Tonight I'm loaded!" Mark helped me up grandly.

We rolled in style through a series of quiet squares—Savannah was a city of squares, Mark told me, each with its own private wrought-iron fenced garden—and I felt as if we'd stepped back into the pages of Gone with the Wind. In the darkness the tall pale pink houses glowed. The mist had risen, and I shivered slightly.

"You're getting wet." Mark took off his silky gray-and-black tweed jacket and draped it round my shoulders. He didn't take his arm away. I didn't say he should.

We rattled over the cobblestones back to the dock area. And right away that sensation of being watched was back. I straightened, and Mark looked at me. "What's the matter?"

"I don't know . . . it feels like someone's following me."

"That's crazy. Who's here who would know you? Not Catriona!" Mark's eyes crinkled knowingly. "Probably some guy envying me for being out with such a fox. Ignore it." He pulled me over to the stores for some window-shopping.

We wandered along the whole dockside area, which by now was jammed. The shops were a fun mixture of expensive merchandise, lovely ethnic items, and tourist junk. "Don't buy anything here. Get Zippórah or Catriona to take you right to the makers," he said as I looked at a reed basket. "Or I'll take you."

I turned to look at him, about to say something about his not having the time, and our eyes met. My heart turned over. All at once I was breathing hard, and he was too.

"Come on," Mark said huskily, taking my elbow, "let's go hear some jazz." And the spell was broken.

The jazz club was much like the restaurant where we'd eaten, only bigger, darker, and more filled with smoke. It was also crowded. My eyes stung as Mark pushed me ahead of him toward a table. "You hold our seats. I'll go to the bar and get our orders before the next set starts. What do you want?"

"Oh . . . a soft drink, anything."

Mark returned with brimming mugs. "Root beer. It's the real thing, made special for this place, and they're famous for it." The root beer was strong with sassafras.

Up on the little platform a tall thin black man slid onto a high stool and lifted his trumpet. Four or five other musicians joined him. The sound was part jazz, part blues, but with a bittersweet undertone like nothing I'd heard before. Unconsciously I was rocking to the rhythm. Mark's arm went around my waist, and my head rested against his shoulder. It was all one, the smoke and the sound and the touch of Mark's hand, and the crispness of his black shirt against my cheek. Then, like a dark thread of foreshadowing in music, that awareness of being watched came creeping in.

I stirred and straightened, and Mark looked at me. "Getting bored?"

"No. I'm—kind of tired. Shouldn't we be going?"

"When the set's over. I'll get you another root beer. That'll keep you awake." He smiled, and slipped out of his seat and over to the bar.

I sat alone at the small table, and found myself shivering.

All the time, the sound of that trumpet went on, exquisitely lonely. I shook myself and looked around, wondering what was taking Mark so long. The bar was long and crowded. I could not find Mark. And then, inexorably, my eyes felt drawn to the bar's far end.

A man in his late twenties was sitting there, his back to the bar. He was looking, not at the musicians, but straight at me. He was dark-blond and deeply tanned, and there was an expression in his eyes—even through the smoke and dimness I could see it. It wasn't as if he were trying to pick me up. I could have handled that, I told myself, grasping for sophistication. This was something different, unreadable. But I couldn't take my eyes away.

Suddenly, to my horror, he slid down from the stool and started toward me.

Chapter Seven

Panic rose in me. Then, blessedly, I heard Mark's familiar voice. "Let's skip the root beer. The bar's too busy. Come on."

He was back to his old curtness, and his hand on my arm was firm. For once I didn't mind. Gratefully I let him hurry me out of the club and toward the *Silver Cat*.

By now the mist had turned into a faint drizzle. The boat floated quietly at its moorings. "Watch yourself," Mark said. "She'll be slippery from the mist." He helped me over the side. The deck, if that's what you called it, certainly was damp and so were the white cushions. I ducked, as Mark suggested, down into the little cabin.

There was a mohair throw on one of the two bunks, and I snuggled into it gratefully. "Come on down and dry off," I started to call up to Mark. Then I heard the voices.

One of them was Mark's. The other was male, and a stranger's. He must have come aboard after us—no, the boat had not shifted with additional weight. He was standing on the dock, and he was angry. Both voices were pitched with anger, though the mist muffled what both speakers were already trying to keep confined to whispers.

Only a few phrases stood out. "—told you that was the end of it," Mark said heatedly. "I had enough when—" The rest was lost when a sudden breeze sent a gust of rain against the cabin windows.

And then the stranger's voice, with a sardonic laugh: "—don't think it's as easy as that, do you? If I started talking—"

"Try it," Mark said, deadly quiet. His tone sent a shudder through me. That broke my paralysis. I bolted, not up the steps, but to the little window above the sink.

The dock was dark, and foggy, but I saw the fluorescent beam from a lamppost pick out a figure. It was the dark-blond man who had been staring so insistently at me from the bar.

Abruptly, like a kaleidoscope shifting, the picture broke. The stranger laughed again and disappeared, whistling, into the dark. Mark clattered down the steps in a foul mood.

"It's building up to a storm. We've got to get going. Dig a poncho out of the bin under the right bunk for me."

I got one not just for him but for myself as well. Mark stared. "What do you think you're going to do?"

"Sit in the cockpit with you. I want to see the storm. And don't tell me I can't. This isn't even your boat." That wasn't diplomatic, but I was not about to admit I wanted him close to me. Not for romantic reasons. I was frightened.

Maybe he knew it somehow. All he said was

"Buckle your seat belt. And hang on. This could be choppy."

We roared out of the harbor as if demons, or maybe the police, were chasing us. I shot a look behind us. A figure had emerged out of the blackness and was standing under the lamp as if watching.

"Who was that?" I said involuntarily.

"Who?" Mark demanded, startled.

"The man you were talking to at the dock."

"You're crazy. I wasn't talking to anyone."

"Yes, you were. I heard you." I saw Mark frown, and I repeated the phrases that I'd heard. "I looked out the window, and I saw him. It was a guy who was staring at me at the jazz club."

Mark looked angry. "That's what it was about," he said at last. "He wanted to know who you were, and I told him to blast off. If he bothers you again, you let me know."

"Was it about your friend Cuffy?" That was a shot in the dark.

"*No!* Cuffy's got nothing to do with this. I don't know who this creep was."

You're lying, I thought silently. I glanced at Mark. He was intent on his navigating, his lips tight.

For the rest of the rocky trip to the island we didn't speak.

Dorr Island lay in pitch-blackness when we arrived. Bonne Espérance was invisible in the distance. Mark tied the boat securely and lifted me out. With our arms round each other we ran blindly up the drive. At last the house loomed.

"Skip the steps. They're slippery." Mark fumbled in his pocket and produced a heavy key to the door between them. It opened into the basement regions I had not yet seen. He struck a match and lit a hanging lantern.

Its frail glow illumined a world of some three hundred years ago. Heavy, rough-stone walls, green with mold and very thick; cracked flagstone floors; bolted, crude wood doors. Mark pulled our ponchos off and flung them to the floor. Then, his arm again round me, he guided me to narrow stairs.

At their foot he stopped. "Look, what you thought you heard. Don't say anything about it. Cat'll only get mad at me for letting you in for it, and it was nothing."

"I didn't 'think' I heard it. And it wasn't nothing."

"For cripe's sake! What are you trying to do, manufacture sinister plots the way your father's doing?"

"What does that mean?"

"That book he's writing. All these crazy C.I.A.– type activities he's supposed to have been involved in —about Americans plotting to overthrow foreign governments. You can't tell me that's all true! Or suppose it is, and suppose you're right about that guy tonight threatening—it was probably because of things your dad's done or knows. Because you're his daughter. So don't try to rationalize the blame onto me and Cuffy!"

I stared at him, unable to believe my ears. Was he trying to throw me off about the man at the docks? Did he resent my father? Was he trying to warn me about Dad's book? I was only sure of one thing—our date had ended as badly as it started, and I still didn't know why.

He gave me a slight push. "Go on up and tell Catriona we got back okay," he said hoarsely. "I have stuff to do here."

He turned away to hang up our ponchos as I went dazedly up the stairs into light and warmth.

Catriona's sitting room was dark, but a thin sliver of light showed beneath her closed bedroom door. I called out softly, "Catriona?"

Her voice came back quietly. "Yes."

"It's me, Tracy. We're back," I whispered, and went on around the double stairwell to my own room. I didn't say anything about being okay.

Chapter Eight

I didn't feel any presence in my room that night, and I didn't dream. I fell asleep far more quickly than I expected, and again, when I awoke, the sun was shining.

I dressed and ran downstairs, my heart doing flip-flops. How was Mark going to behave—how was I going to behave—after the way we'd parted? I took a deep breath and went into the dining room.

It was deserted. There was no trace of breakfast on the table. Frowning, I pushed open the door to the silent kitchen, and Catriona's voice hailed me from the gallery.

"Who is that? Mark or Tracy?"

"It's your wicked stepdaughter," I said flippantly. Apparently I'd have a few more minutes to get my act together before facing Mark, and I felt relieved.

Catriona was sitting at the table on the back gallery, eating bread and cheese and drinking coffee. She pushed the cheese board toward me. "Help yourself. Zipporah still isn't feeling well, and I made her stay in bed. Behind her back I'm reverting to my European eating habits. There's still coffee in the pot, I think."

I poured some and cut a hunk of cheese. "Has Mark gone off already?"

"Mark," Catriona said, "is still in bed. What time did you two get home anyway?"

"Late. I called to you."

"Yes, I know." Catriona's tone was abstracted, and it dawned on me that something was wrong. I looked at her, and at the same moment her eyes, too, lifted. I started to ask what happened, and at the same time she said, "Tracy, did you see anyone around as you two came back here?"

"Around? You mean, here on Dorr Island?" Catriona nodded, and I shook my head. "I didn't notice anything much at all. I think I would have though, if—" My mind focused. "Do you mean there was a prowler? Here?"

"There might have been. Tracy, what exactly made you say you could have sworn someone was in the room with you the night before last?"

Catriona's exact repetition of my own words startled me, and so did the seriousness in her eyes. "I woke up feeling like someone was in the room," I said soberly. "When I got the light on, no one was there. Or on the galleries, or on the lawn either. I couldn't see anything moving in the woods. But the—the seat of the love seat was warm, as though someone had been sitting on it. Even though I'd seen no one there. Catriona, was somebody prowling around last night while we were away?"

"I was awake, reading in the sitting room," Catriona said with a scientist's exactness. "I heard a sound."

"What? Music?" I asked involuntarily.

Catriona looked puzzled. "No. Something rustling. Then I had that same sensation you did, that someone was in the house. Not Zipporah. The prescription she took would have knocked her out, and anyway, I'd know her step. I had the impression someone was outside. I put the light out, and went to the gallery." She pointed to the one above our heads. "It was empty, just as it was for you. I thought I heard something down here."

"You didn't come down!" I exclaimed.

"No. I got your father's gun out of the armoire" I blinked at that "and sat in the dark waiting till I heard you two come in." Catriona looked at me. "I came down as soon as it was light this morning. There was no sign of a break-in. There wouldn't be; the French windows are always left open in the summer. But I could swear those papers your father left on the library table had been disturbed."

"We'd better call the police." I started to rise. Catriona caught my arm.

"No." She said it evenly, quietly. But there was a note in her voice that made me stop, open-mouthed.

"Catriona, you can't just ignore this! We've got to report it. If you feel silly calling the police, let's get Mark down here to take a look around."

"No," Catriona said again. "Just you and me. That's why I've let him and Zipporah sleep. You and I must check the house, especially the library, and find out what if anything's been tampered with. I know how to search. I'm trained to examine sites for traces the ordinary layman would miss."

"Why not have Mark help?" I repeated, my own self-consciousness forgotten. "He helps with your work; you said so."

"Because it's your father's work, not mine, that's been gone through. That's why we can't bring the police in," Catriona said, as if that explained everything. I did a double take.

"Catriona, Mark told me all this crazy stuff about Dad's book. Don't tell me it's *true!* About C.I.A. activities—and counterespionage—and American nationals plotting secretly to overthrow foreign dictatorships . . ."

Birds were singing, and insects buzzed in the wisteria vines, and Catriona just sat there, looking at me out of those dark eyes. I sat down weakly.

"*Catriona.*"

"You'll have to ask your father about all that. I can't tell you. But if you mean could anyone have reason to try to prevent your father's book from being published, yes. That's why we're not telling anyone about any of this. Your father must be the one to decide whether to take it further. I think from now on we'd better keep the French doors locked at night. I'll call Savannah and have a burglar-alarm system installed. I can say it's to protect the Dulaine antiques and artifacts." Catriona paused. "Now, are you going to help me make the search, or not?"

We went through the house from roof level to cellar, and apart from my getting to see the locked storerooms, the wine cellar, and Catriona's "museum storage," nothing was significant. I even had to admit that the papers Catriona had referred to, which to my eyes might as well have been in code, could easily have been rustled and disarranged by last night's rainstorm. The wind had been heavy when Mark and I crossed the water and ran up the drive.

"That's that, then," Catriona said when we finished a second inspection of the library and study. I couldn't tell whether she was dissatisfied or relieved. She took all of the materials Dad had left on the desk and tables and locked them in a hidden cupboard in the paneling. "We've been through everything except Mark's room, and I don't have to worry about inspecting that! If he finds anything disturbed, he'll yell bloody murder. And you've provided him with an alibi for all last evening." She saw the expression in my eyes and added swiftly, "That was a joke."

But I was remembering what Catriona and Zipporah had both said, about Mark and his earlier wildness, Mark and his secrets. He was keeping secrets right now, and I knew it, if my stepmother did not.

We came out into the hall just as the malachite clock behind us struck eleven. "About time we got Mark up anyway," Catriona murmured. "At this rate none of us are going to do any work today!" She turned to me and smiled. "Thanks for making the rounds with me. And for not making me feel foolish."

"*You* feel foolish!" I smiled back. "At least now I don't feel like I'm the only one making up midnight visitors. Or conjuring up the ghost of St. Pierre's murder victim, or something!"

"So you've found out about that story already, have you? Don't breathe a word of any of this in front of Zipporah, or we'll start hearing how my archaeological digging has 'waked the *Chat d'Argent*,' " Catriona murmured wryly. I had my mouth already open to ask what the quote meant when she turned toward the hall's center table and frowned.

"Somebody must have brought the mail up from the dock while we were in the cellar. Or else Mark has taken off again and left a note."

She walked toward the inlaid table with its bronze lady holding candles and its Chinese brocade mat.

I didn't hear a creaking or a tinkling. I swear I didn't hear anything except the slap of her espadrilles on the Oriental rug, and the insects in the wisteria, and the distant, incessant sound of the salt marsh sighing. But *something* made me cry out, *"Look out!"* even as I looked up and saw the heavy malachite, brass, and crystal chandelier begin to sway.

In slow motion I saw the crystal prisms clashing against each other, saw the whole heavy mass swing and revolve on the velvet-covered chain that stretched endlessly up into the skylight dome. Saw the velvet fray, and the chain give way.

I threw myself at Catriona, knocking her to the floor, just as the chandelier came crashing down.

Chapter Nine

Catriona fell sideways, and I fell with her, onto the threadbare velvet rug. The chandelier fell at an angle, too, so that it landed not on the center table but beside it. *Right where Catriona had been standing*, my mind thought numbly. It mostly missed us, except that one bronze candlebranch gave me a tremendous whack on my right ankle, and the circular bronze frame had cut into Catriona's left leg. Her red blood seeped into a red-brown pattern in the carpet, and disappeared.

For a moment we both just sprawled there. Then Catriona sat up shakily. "Thank goodness the darn thing didn't land on the table! Grandfather always said it's one of the most valuable things around here. It's *piètre dure*, you know. . . ."

She was in shock, rambling. "Shut up and stay put," I told her, and then yelled, "*Mark!*"

His voice answered urgently, "*Tracy?*" and his feet came pounding. Not down from upstairs. From outdoors, up the entrance steps. He burst in the front

57

door, shouting, "What the hell's happening?" And stopped dead.

"See for yourself," I said tartly, pulling myself with difficulty to my feet. My ankle was throbbing. Mark took a comprehensive look and then, since Catriona was bleeding but clearly had no major bones broken, scooped her up and carried her into the library.

"Not the sofa! I can't bleed on that priceless old upholstery!" Catriona protested, proving she was feeling better. Mark ignored that. I grabbed newspapers to put between her leg and the blue silk velvet. Mark laid her down and examined her leg with surprising expertise.

"You were darn lucky. I told you that old piece of junk was a hazard. If you weren't going to have it fixed, you should have sold it. It's a clean cut, but deep. It needs stitches. You up to a boat ride into town, or you want me to call a doctor to come out here?"

"Neither. And that chandelier's not a piece of junk. If it were, it wouldn't be worth anything. Anyway, Ken did fix it. I don't want a doctor. Go down to Zipporah and get some bandages and antiseptic; she's bound to have them. And don't tell her what really happened," Catriona said sternly. "I don't want her up here. Make up a story. You're good at that."

"Yes, ma'am," Mark said with mock humility. He went. I got water and a clean white dish towel from the kitchen, and began to wash Catriona's wound. "What's *pietre dure*?" I asked her to take her mind off the near catastrophe.

"Petrified wood, only it's not wood, really, it's marble and malachite and lapis and a lot of other semiprecious stones. It's what's called a specimen table. World travelers like St. Pierre used to have them made, one specimen piece of every gemstone they'd picked up on their journeys. . . ."

All the time she was talking, a flock of suspicious and unanswered questions wheeled like birds inside my head.

Mark came back. Zipporah was with him. She thrust both Mark and me out of the way unceremoniously and took over. To my astonishment, after sponging the cut with alcohol and peroxide, Zipporah laid a handful of dull green leaves over it before reaching for the bandage. "Don't give me no argument, young lady. Yarrow poultice always drew out the infection when you was a child, and it still do."

She added something under her breath in Gullah, and Catriona answered, equally sharply though still in a whisper. Then, the bandage neatly applied, Zipporah straightened.

"All right, what happen? Don't make up no nonsense. I got eyes, and this here didn't happen while you all be messing around with no scholarly studies."

Catriona and Mark exchanged glances. Then Catriona gave a very effective laugh. "It's nothing. The hall chandelier finally broke loose. I guess the steel cable Ken ran up through the chain wasn't strong enough after all. No real harm's done. The table hasn't got a scratch. Some of the chandelier's malachite broke off, and a lot of prisms, but it's fixable. I guess when its time came to fall, it had to fall. Even I wasn't hurt badly, thanks to Tracy. She saw what was happening in time."

"Nobody could've *seen* in time." Zipporah turned and gave me a long, searching glance that made me shiver. Then she swung back. She'd put herself between me and Catriona and Mark, so that the three of them formed a closed Dorr Island triangle. "Don't tell me nothing about its being St. Pierre's chandelier's time! You know whats time it is! '*Faut ne réveiller pas le Chat d'Argent!*' "

"*Tante Zipporah! Tais-toi, ou—*" Mark lapsed into a spate of Gullah. Whatever it meant, it worked. Zipporah's face went gray. She fingered something on a cord around her neck, shot a glance in my direction, and went, her expression thunderous.

"Thanks," Catriona said weakly. Now that the crisis was over, she looked wan. "Look, would you two guys please clean up the mess? I don't want anyone else seeing it and invoking the shadow of the cat. Get a carton, and put all the pieces in carefully. Then lock it in the cellar. I'll have to find someplace that will restore it."

She fished in her pocket for her key ring. Mark seemed about to reach for it, but she tossed it to me. I went to the kitchen, and Zipporah gave me a broom and dustpan. Mark came back from the cellar with a huge wooden crate. "This will be heavy to drag downstairs, but it's the best thing." We gathered up the loose prisms and pieces of prisms, the pieces of marble-like bright green malachite, and wrapped them carefully in tissue paper. I was again astonished at the sensitive dexterity of Mark's fingers. Then, together, we lifted the heavy chandelier frame and deposited it in the box. Mark gathered up the velvet-covered chain and began to coil it neatly. I heard him catch his breath.

"What is it?" I asked immediately.

"Darn steel cable sliced my finger. It's nothing; it's not even bleeding. Look, we ought to wrap this monstrosity in protective padding. Run up to the linen cupboard, will you? It's the big armoire outside the bathroom. There's an old striped cotton quilt in there."

I ran and found it, and when I ran back down, Mark had the chain and its accessories neatly coiled in a corner of the box. We tucked the blanket carefully in around everything, and then we dragged the crate down the narrow cellar stairs. It was a slow, painstaking, and difficult job. At last the crate was in Catriona's "museum," underneath one of the sawhorse display tables. Mark locked the door after us and pointedly handed me the key. "Here. Catriona appointed you the official keeper."

"Mark, don't be like that."

"Oh, I don't care. Just because my cousin prefers to trust a new stepdaughter who's a perfect stranger over her own blood kin. . . . Sorry," Mark added swiftly, "nothing personal intended. You're right, I am acting like a spoiled brat. I'm also ready to explode, so I'd better get out of here. You coming?" He waited for me to precede him.

Catriona was waiting for us. "I'm sorry, I have a splitting headache. It's a gorgeous day out, and the storm may have washed some artifacts loose in the slave quarters. Would you two go work there a couple of hours without me?"

"After lunch," I said firmly, glancing at the clock. "No wonder you have a headache! You must be starved." It was already two o'clock. I went to the kitchen and found Zipporah fixing lunch and muttering to herself. We ate in the library, on the theory that it was the only way to keep Catriona off her leg. Afterward Mark asked if I was ready for some fieldwork, and I said, "You go ahead. I'll catch up with you in half an hour."

I stayed in my room, half hidden by a curtain, till I saw Mark go striding through the backyard in the direction of the dig. Then, Catriona's keys still in my pocket, I crept cautiously down to the cellar.

Even with the electricity on, it was dim and musty. I unlocked the door to the museum and went in, closing the door behind me. Then I knelt down on the floor of cobblestones and hard-packed earth, and uncovered the chandelier. I felt around the corners till I found the chain and pulled it out.

I looked, as I'd seen Mark look, and my breath caught like his. It shouldn't have. I'd been half expecting what I saw. The old brass chain had worn through and separated, but the shiny new cable my father had installed had not broken. It had not come uncoupled. The end was neither frayed, nor clean-cut for coupling; it was half of each. As if someone had deliberately cut partway through, and left time and the chandelier's weight to do the rest.

Chapter Ten

I sensed, rather than quite heard, a footfall behind me. I turned. Zipporah stood like an implacable Fate in the open doorway, her arms folded. She looked at me, and I looked at her, and she said, "Best you all got away from here. You and your father, and Miss Catriona too."

"Bonne Espérance is Catriona's home!"

"Did I say it wasn't?" Zipporah retorted blandly. "Your father, he a big writer now, he got money. You and your father, you make Miss Cat leave *L'Isle d'Or*. Just for a time. Just till the autumn. Till the Cat sleep again."

"Zipporah, what *is* this about the Silver Cat? What does it mean, and what wakes it?"

Zipporah looked at me gravely. "It not be for me to tell. You not of the island."

"You mean, I'm an outsider. But I'm Catriona's stepdaughter. And she's in danger. Bonne Espérance is in danger, isn't it? Zipporah, tell me!"

"That would be bad bad. It displease the spirits.

It be a Dulaine must tell you. You get your papa back here, and make him make *her* tell you. Make her go." Zipporah's eyes bored into me, and her speech became markedly Gullah. "Silver Cat walk in your room be warning. *This* be warning. Blood go be cry out for blood on de island, an' my baby be hurt if she stay too college-proud to listen. *You* have gifts. *You* make her listen."

As quickly and silently as she had come, she was gone.

Considerably shaken, I locked up the cellars and crept upstairs. I didn't tell any of this to Catriona. In our absence she'd dragged herself out to the gallery and was dozing on the wicker chaise longue. What I did do was go into the library, and Catriona's study, and root through address books and correspondence till I found the telephone number of Dad's publisher. Zipporah was right; he should be here.

Forty minutes and innumerable phone calls later, I gave up in dismay. Dad had reached Washington, but he'd already left—or at least he'd left the hotel he'd given his editor as a contact point. The editor had suggested a number of people to try at various government agencies, but they had either not heard from Dad lately or had already speeded him on his way. I left a trail of urgent messages, and took down an equal number of messages for him.

At last, there being nothing else I could think of to do, I went out to the dig. The sun was still blazing, but lower in the sky, and a faint breeze stirred. Mark was squatting on the earth, his shirt off, the muscles in his bronzed back rippling. He was carefully brushing dirt off a number of fresh pottery shards. I went over and sat down cross-legged, not too near him, and we worked in silence for a time. After a while he looked up and grinned.

"Looks like the storm last night kicked up quite a bit." He wasn't talking about artifacts alone, and we both knew it.

I smiled back, a trifle shakily. "I don't feel much like talking right now, okay? I've got a lot to think about."

"So have I." We returned to silence, a warmer silence now.

There was a rustling in the woods, and a little girl emerged. She was about seven or eight, and her skin was a purple-black, and she was beautiful. "Yo, Mark," she said politely, and stood waiting, well back from the edge of the dig. Mark looked up, and his face split in a smile.

"Yo, Sophra. What brings you here?"

She answered in a soft flood of liquid, singsong Gullah in which the only words I could recognize were *Cuffy* and *Zipporah*. Mark spoke to her once, sharply. She answered. Then he turned to me. "I have to go see a guy. On the island. I'll be right back. You'll be all right here without me, won't you?"

"Of course, I will." I wouldn't have admitted if I had been nervous, and actually I was not. Compared to what had happened in the house this morning, the slave quarters seemed peaceful, and the fresh air a blessing. I continued to work on alone, and the area's mysterious tranquillity became more intense. After a while I heard a rustling sound again, and I looked up, my senses all alert. Then I laughed with a mixture of relief and pleasure.

A peacock was stepping out of the forest, assertive and curious. He looked back at me and then, deliberately, unfurled his tail. Strutting with an arrogance that made me think of Mark, he picked his way into the dig, scanned the scratched soil, and carefully selected a choice grub. Then he gave me a sideways look and flicked his tail.

I laughed aloud, and he bowed gravely. He did a kind of little dance, scratching and pouncing on grubs while I watched, enchanted. He was not at all disconcerted at my presence, and I remembered what I'd read somewhere, how peacocks were now native wildlife in a lot of southern areas as a result of having been brought generations ago to adorn grand plantations.

That was obviously what had happened on Dorr Island. *He* was the native, and I the visitor, and when he started to stroll off again, I couldn't bear to let him go. Mark could not have gone far; he would be back at any minute, and if I stuck to the well-trodden path, I surely couldn't get into any trouble.

I scrambled up and followed the peacock out of the slave quarters. I kept on following, down the grassy path between dark frames of forest, as the sun sank lower. It dazzled my eyes, making a golden path like a yellow-brick road.

Presently I found myself in a little clearing, infinitely melancholy, and the peacock had disappeared. A tabby wall and chimney stood there; like the ones I'd noticed at the ruined slave cabins, they were garlanded with roses. This building had been larger than the slave cabins though; I could make out the outlines of several rooms. There were the remains of an elaborate door frame, atop a series of three shallow steps. I sat down on the center one and reached out toward the sweetness of one of the old roses.

Darn! I thought, as thorns scratched me. One of the thorns had grabbed my watchband, and as I jerked my arm away a whole thicket of rose branches bent with it, away from the doorstep—

I looked down and froze.

There, where the low-swooping branches had been covering it, was a carved outline, incomplete but unmistakable. The outline of a crouching cat.

Carefully, I groped around for a fallen branch, *not* from a rosebush. Carefully, I used the branch to hold back the other thorny ones. I unhooked myself and searched for other tree branches to cage the rosebush harmlessly away. Then I knelt down and, with the delicacy Catriona had taught me to use with artifacts, I brushed the loose dirt of years out of the carving.

A newly awakened cat, carved with elegant economy, glared back at me. It was framed with a kind of twisted border of swords and ribbons. A streamer above the cat's head bore the legend: *Il faut ne réveiller pas le Chat d'Argent.* And below, in a flattened oval, the name: DULAINE.

Wake not the Silver Cat. The family motto, and the family crest.

I sat back on my heels, at once relieved and half deflated. A cloud covered the sun, and the air turned gray and chilly. Mark would be worried. I'd better be getting back, whether he had returned or not. I released the rosebush from its confinement, and it sprang back to cover the carving once again. Then I turned and, very carefully, made my way back toward the slave quarters.

It wasn't long before I had an alarming feeling that I had lost my way. I should have reached the quarters by now. Worse, the path had grown narrower and the sun, what was left of it, was coming from the wrong direction.

And then it came, suddenly, silently—that sense that I was being watched and followed. I began walking faster, and then I started running, knowing only that if I stopped, I would be too paralyzed to move. I came to a fork in the path and chose one, haphazardly, out of a primitive instinct. And the presence in the woods went with me.

It wasn't threatening. It was, somehow, warning me. What had Zipporah said? That everything so far had been a warning, that death was coming, and blood would have blood.

My heart was pounding, and I could scarcely see. Then, horribly, my ankle turned, and I plunged over. Not down on the path, but sideways. Over the path edge, down into the swamp.

The secret wet world Catriona had warned me of seethed beneath the deceptive sea of reeds and undergrowth. Wet slime engulfed me. I screamed and struggled. And the word I screamed, over and over again, was Mark's name.

He was answering. He was coming. He was *there*, plunging into the swamp and engulfing me. His arms went around me, and he pulled me out. It sounds so quick and easy when I tell it, but it wasn't. And then I was lying on the high, dry path, and his arms were around me.

My arms went up around his neck, convulsively, and we clung together. Then he was kissing me. I was kissing him, as if we couldn't stop.

Something had happened, more than my fall in the swamp, and we both knew it. I'd never felt this way about a boy before. But I found myself wondering how I could kiss Mark like that when I knew I didn't quite trust him. I wasn't afraid of him. It wasn't that. I just knew that he was keeping secrets from me.

Briefly I wondered what he saw in *me*. He could make me feel so young and naive. Yet I knew that for him, as for me, something—irrevocably—had happened.

Chapter Eleven

There was a spell over Bonne Espérance, and the name of the spell was secrecy. I knew it, and as days went by it bothered me increasingly. Knew, too, that I was part of it—I wasn't just surrounded by secrets; I was keeping a few of my own.

When Mark took me back to the big house after our meeting at the swamp, he guided me up the outside stairs and around the gallery, past the windows of empty rooms, till I reached my own. We didn't discuss that; it was a case of two minds with a single thought, and the thought was that there was no reason to alarm Catriona with the news of my falling in.

Whatever, I sneaked inside, and took a badly needed bath, and came down to a dinner at which both Mark and I acted as if nothing out of the ordinary had occurred. And later I ran my stinking, swamp-soaked clothes through the washer and dryer, and said nothing about that either. Maybe Catriona noticed something in the way Mark and I looked, or didn't look, at one another. But if so, she said nothing about it either.

I didn't tell Catriona about the ruined cottage I had found, but the next day, when we were working together in the study, I said casually, "*Wake not the Silver Cat*'s the Dulaine family motto, isn't it? Where did it come from? Old St. Pierre?"

Catriona shook her head. "A lot of people think so, hereabouts, and with reason. St. Pierre had a—a special whip—" She bit her lip. "Oh, let's be honest, the man was a brute and a sadist, and whether he deliberately murdered that poor girl or not, he certainly was responsible indirectly for her death. And for others too. Whoever owns one of these great plantations, just like the owner of a business, is ultimately responsible for whatever happens on it."

She's speaking in the present tense, not the past, my mind noted and instinctively filed away. Catriona seemed not to notice as she went on. "St. Pierre had a silver-handled whip—not a riding crop, like all the gentry carried, but a cat-o'-nine-tails like the ones used in those days to discipline insubordinate sailors. Or slaves. Each of the whip's nine thongs had a sharp metal tip; in St. Pierre's case, silver."

I flinched involuntarily at the picture this conjured, and Catriona nodded grimly. "Horrible, isn't it? It's no wonder there were slave uprisings. I wouldn't have been surprised if St. Pierre had wound up murdered, but of course, he didn't. Unless there were a way to *scare* someone to death."

"The girl's dying curse."

"Yes. And then of course, there were rumors that turned into legends." Catriona hesitated. "Why am I being so squeamish? It was all more than a hundred and fifty years ago, and anyway, you're helping with my research. And you're part of the family now." She flashed me a warm glance, and I smiled back. "There are two local explanations of the family motto. One that it referred to the whip, and the need not to wake St. Pierre's vicious temper. The other that it was a warning not to arouse divine or spirit retribution on one's evil actions. That started from the girl's curse, and the cat scratches on St. Pierre's body. But the truth is, the motto came with the family from France, where it had been around for a couple of hundred years."

That afternoon Mark ran Catriona and me to Savannah in the *Silver Cat*, and while he went off on business of his own, I drove Catriona to the doctor's. He laughed over Zipporah's leaf poultice as he gave Catriona a tetanus shot and sewed her up, but he said the cut was doing fine.

"Who's to say Zipporah's poultice had nothing to do with that? The lab boys are beginning to find out there's a lot more scientific sense in folk medicine than we used to credit. A lot of it still exists in the Sea Islands, doesn't it? How did you manage to do that to your leg, anyway?"

Catriona, whom I instinctively knew to be deeply truthful, looked him straight in the eye and said calmly, "Oh, pottering around in my dig."

"You're a gardener, hmm? I hear the gardens on Dorr Island used to be spectacular."

Catriona nodded.

There was an aura of secrecy over other things as well. My falling in the swamp remained secret from Catriona. My finding the abandoned cottage and the motto remained a secret, period. I still didn't know when Dad was coming back, where he was, or what he was doing, and I hadn't told Catriona that I'd tried to reach him.

I talked about Dad with Catriona, and I tried to get her to tell me about his work. Apparently she didn't know much more about it than I did, except that it was dangerous and top secret. I talked, deliberately casual, to Catriona about Mark, fishing through what she told me of his background for clues to what he was. I didn't tell Mark about those talks, and Mark wasn't telling either of us where he took off for, like a bat out of hell, at irregular intervals. I couldn't eat a simple meal without feeling that everything Mark and I said had a double meaning. But we didn't bring our attraction out in the open. In my mind I was sure it would never work out between us; I supposed he was telling himself the same thing.

I still hadn't told Catriona the weird elements of our Savannah date. Or about how the cable in the chandelier chain had been half cut through. I should have; I know I should have, but something held me back. I didn't tell anyone, either, about the presence I sensed watching me. Twice more in the night I woke and felt something nonthreatening keeping me company, and once when I was walking back from the slave quarters alone, that presence alerted me to a snake lurking in the grass.

A week and a half went by. Zipporah was over her illness and was clucking like a mother hen and occasionally shouting "Hallelujah!" over Catriona's leg, now healing nicely. I worked with Catriona in the study, and with Catriona and Mark, together, on the dig. Never with Mark alone. One mystery in my life did clear up though. I heard from my mother—a long, wonderfully chatty letter telling me everything she was doing in Argentina. The oil world sounded very high pressure, but she seemed to be thriving on it. Even though I longed to confide in my mother about my mixed feelings for Mark, even though I missed her company, I was glad her new life was working out so well for her.

In late afternoons Catriona took me on tours of the island, on foot or in the carriage. I met Mr. Rafiel Jones, who was in Gullah talk the island's "Man of Words," the local storyteller. And Sister Janie Ruth Ford, whom you could call a woman of words, because she was the island preacher. And a lot of other people—fishers or small farmers or craftspeople who worked over on the mainland, going back and forth in their own small boats. All of them had musical voices and enormous dignity, all of them were descendants of Dorr Island slaves. I was welcomed graciously, but beneath their courteous manner and soft tones was a reserve that indicated clearly I was an outsider.

I said as much when Catriona told me I should feel free to go back on my own, and she laughed. "I grew up here, at least summers, and I'm a Dulaine, but *I'm* an outsider too. Not as much as a mainlander, or heaven forbid, a northerner, but still!"

"I'm a mainlander—*and* from the Midwest. . . ."

"Yes, but you and your father are now Dorr Islanders by marriage." Catriona turned to smile at me as the carriage jolted slowly through the sunset light. "That makes you belong. Not as much as if you were born here, or a Gullah. But nearly as much as I do."

"How about Mark?"

"I've been thinking," Catriona went on as smoothly as if I hadn't spoken. "It's a shame for you to be tied to the big house because you don't know your way around the marshes. I keep being busy, and heaven knows where Mark disappears to! Shadow knows exactly where it's safe to step." She gave the horse's gray rump an affectionate pat. "You could go round alone if you took Shadow and the carriage. Or—do you ever ride?"

"I used to, at my grandfather's farm."

"Why don't you take him out for a ramble on your own after work tomorrow?"

"Mark's taking me in to Savannah."

I said it matter-of-factly, but I blushed, and Catriona gave me a knowing, sisterly look. But she said only a noncommittal "Oh, that's nice."

Actually we were going not just for the sightseeing Mark recommended, but for dinner. It had been Mark's idea, produced brusquely when Catriona had briefly left us alone together at the dig that morning. He'd blurted it out as if he hadn't thought it through, and half regretted it, and I'd accepted in just about the same way. "I've got to go out at dawn on a fishing trip the next day, so we won't stay out late," he'd added, and I'd said, "Good." And that was the extent of our romantic conversation.

Mark didn't show up for dinner that night. "He and Cuffy, dey go out in *Chat d'Argent*. Mm-hmmm," Zipporah said with disapproval. I suspected he stayed out all night, for in the grayness before sunrise the next morning I heard the hum of a fast boat approaching the island, and soon after that the sound of feet climbing the outside stairs. He was not at breakfast, or at lunch, and when I went down to the dock, where we'd agreed to meet at three o'clock, neither Mark nor the *Silver Cat* were there.

The little girl who'd come to get Mark that afternoon at the dig was dangling her bare feet in the water. "Mark, he got a job to do in *Chat d'Argent*. He not come back till late late," she said firmly.

Maybe he'd thought better of our going out alone. Maybe I was thinking better of it too. I went back to Bonne Espérance, changed into jeans, and went out to saddle up Shadow. I'd go exploring as Catriona had suggested, and if Mark returned, he could just find me if he wanted to go to Savannah with me.

I knew where I wanted to go, and it was not back to Mr. Rafiel Jones's or Sister Janie's. That abandoned cottage drew me. I guided Shadow past the slave quarters and down the path where the peacock had led me. The peacocks appeared, a whole flock of them, picking their way disdainfully around Shadow's legs. Shadow ignored them. He knew exactly where he was heading, and I let him have his way. The sun was beating down through the gap the trail made through the trees. It was hot on my head and shoulders, both of which were bare. I felt a little giddy, probably because I hadn't eaten much at lunch on account of the upcoming dinner in Savannah. Or maybe I was just suffering culture shock as a result of a lot of things. I rocked along on Shadow's back, and Shadow's gentle jog and the sun on the peacock's iridescent feathers dazzled me. I was *not* watching where we were going. Because when Shadow came into a clearing, and stopped, it took me several minutes to realize the cottage in front of me was not the cottage of the Dulaine motto.

For one thing, it wasn't ruined, only very shabby. For another, it stood amid gardens like those you see in pictures of Shakespeare's England. Plants flowered waist-high in beds bisected by neat paths of oyster-shells. The hum of bees was everywhere, and an intoxicating fragrance. *I've gotten back on the Gullah side of the island after all*, I thought.

Then I realized that the girl gathering flowers in the garden was white. She wore an ankle-length dress, like the Laura Ashley ones I've coveted in vain, and her hair—so pale a blond, it was almost white—hung longer than her waist, held by a velvet band. She was singing to herself, in a sweet high voice, an old English ballad I'd learned in school chorale.

Shadow neighed and snorted, and the girl straightened. She was shorter than I, but about my age, I thought with pleasure. Suddenly the idea of a girlfriend, somebody from my own world, on Dorr Island, was enormously appealing.

Then she turned, and it was as if a cloud passed across the sun. As I had the night I'd awakened to the presence in my room, I felt cold. And I understood the Gullah use of double adjectives for emphasis. Because this wasn't a girl in front of me at all. And it wasn't a currently fashionable Laura Ashley dress. The dress, and the woman wearing it, were *old old*.

Chapter Twelve

The spooked sensation lasted only for a second. Then the little woman was coming toward me, her wrinkled face lighting with pleasure.

"You must be the new girl over at Bonne Espérance. How nice! I so rarely have guests for tea anymore." Her voice was sweet and high, very southern. "Hello, Shadow. How are you today, old boy?" She stroked his forehead and he nuzzled her pocket till he found a sugar cube. He was used to coming here, I thought. Then she turned back to me, eagerly.

"Do come down—I'm sorry, there's no mounting-block here, but you can manage, can't you? I used to, when I still rode. Tell me, is Zipporah's migraine any better? I tried a different tea for that this time, and I've been worried, because she hasn't been back."

Of course, I thought, my mind clearing. This must be the herb lady Zipporah got her folk remedies from! I didn't know why I was so surprised to find she wasn't Gullah. I climbed down, feeling insanely as though I ought to curtsy.

"You're Tracy Fairbrother, Catriona Dulaine's stepdaughter, and you've moved here from the Midwest, and you're helping her with her work. I hope you can keep her from disturbing the spirits." I blinked, but the little woman went on as matter-of-factly as Zipporah. "Of course, there's a fifty-fifty chance that what she's doing is good good. Dulaines are always intensely spiritual or intensely evil." For a minute a shadow went across her face. Then it lighted again, and she patted my hand.

"Let us sit in the moon garden, and you can tell me what it is like for you to move to our Sea Islands. I call it my moon garden because it's all white flowers. Many of them night-flowering. Poor St. Pierre's wife, the one he drove into an early grave, loved white flowers, you know, and I've planted this garden in her memory. Poor thing, no one ever remembers *her*. It's always St. Pierre and that poor Cat-Marie, whom he killed, everyone talks of."

Talk about culture shock. Things were coming at me too quickly. I could feel myself shaking, and all of a sudden the old lady's hands were gentle but firm upon my arms.

"Now, my dear, you will come sit down. Have you eaten anything? No, I thought not, and you out without a hat in the Georgia sun." She guided me to a wooden bench and sat beside me. "Tracy Fairbrother, you may have an old soul, but you are not yet very wise."

The rational part of my mind was thinking, *Here's where I can find out about St. Pierre and his murders. I wonder why Catriona hasn't talked to her yet.* As if I'd zapped back into a nineteenth-century conversation, I murmured, "You have the advantage of me. You know who I am, but I don't know your name."

She hesitated for a moment. "You may call me Amalie. I'm the herb lady. Now, I have tansy cakes fresh out of the oven, and it won't take a minute to bring the kettle to a boil. You sit here on this bench."

I sat, assailed by the scents of mint and thyme. Amalie went. She returned, carrying a tray with a teapot, a plate of little cakes, and two cracked cups. The tea was sweet and lemon-flavored, the cups didn't leak, and the cakes were very good. I discovered I was ravenous.

I also discovered that after my fourth cake and third cup, I was talking as freely and spontaneously as if my hostess *had* been a girl of my own age. I even spilled out my tumultuous feelings toward Mark.

"You will be good for him," Amalie said. She searched my eyes. "And he for you, so long as you draw him into your world, and not he into his. That would be bad bad. Mark is a Dulaine man; he thinks he knows what is real and important, but he does not always."

"I'm beginning to wonder if I do myself." I put my cup down very carefully in its saucer, because for some reason my eyes weren't focusing too well. "I know Bonne Espérance has secrets. Sometimes I'm sure it has—spirits—in it as well. Only I don't know what they are, or what they're there for."

"The Gullah will tell you the spirits are everywhere. Some bad bad, some good good, some both. Just like people."

"The Gullah won't tell me anything. I'm not an islander." I found myself turning to Amalie earnestly. "That's what I don't understand. If there are spirits, why are they coming to me?"

"Because you have the gifts," Amalie said gravely,

and I remembered Zipporah saying something like that to me in the cellar. I shivered, and Amalie's faded eyes softened. "Gifts are good good, if you use them wisely. Like Mr. Rafiel Jones, or Sister Janie. Or Catriona Dulaine. Not like some others."

"Then you do know Catriona."

"I hear much much about her." Amalie rose. "I regret I have not yet been able to call upon her since she came, so please please, you will not speak to her about our meeting. It has not been proper. *Tu comprends?*"

"Okay," I said reluctantly.

"And now you must go home, because the sun is dying. But you will come call on me again, yes?"

She looked so eager, so like a little girl, that I said "Okay" again, and meant it.

I mounted Shadow, who had been quietly cropping meadow grass, and turned out of the clearing. Amalie was right, I had been out in the sun too long. I was having trouble keeping balance. Fortunately Shadow knew exactly where he should be going. Or so I thought, until he turned into another clearing, and I recognized the roses foaming over a crumbling wall.

He had carried me to the ruined cottage.

"No, Shadow! We're going home. Back to Bonne Espérance." I pulled his left rein, trying to make him turn. He obeyed, but skittishly, doing a little dance.

We're both loopy, I remember thinking. Shadow pranced down what looked like the proper path. There was a scream like a banshee in the woods, and then a peacock emerged, flaunting his tail.

And then, suddenly, Shadow was lurching. His nostrils flared. He turned back toward the cottage, dancing in a circle. "Come on, Shadow. Come *on!*

It's just the peacocks. No matter what anyone says, it isn't spirits. Or if it is, you ought to know them. You're an islander, aren't you?"

I urged Shadow onward, with my hands and my heels, and thought he was quieting again. Then a nightbird cried somewhere in the dark.

I could feel Shadow gathering his muscles beneath me. With a burst of speed he spurted down the path again. And suddenly stumbled over something in the grass.

He screamed, a high-pitched scream, and reared. And I, caught off-guard, flew from the saddle and landed ignominiously in the grass. *Thank goodness it wasn't in the swamp again*, I thought, picking myself up with difficulty. Shadow was vanishing in the distance, a mere gray glimmer.

I could hear the nightbirds, and the sounds of water creatures, as I summoned all my senses to point me in the home direction. I wished passionately that Mark would come looking for me. Where on earth had Mark gone? Why had he stood me up, without any warning?

I was so busy thinking about Mark with my befuddled mind that I didn't look where I was going. I, too, stumbled. Probably over the same darn branch, I thought, my brain clearing. I'd better drag it out of the path before somebody else gets hurt.

I looked down, and everything in me turned *cold cold*.

It wasn't a branch. It was a jean-covered pair of legs.

It was a young black man, lying motionless across the path. I bent and reached for his wrist to check his pulse. And then my lungs and stomach knotted in a soundless scream.

It wasn't just *a* young black man. It was the one who had waited for Mark beneath the Savannah street-light. He had the same earring in his ear, and the same medallion on a chain around his neck.

He was dead, cold dead. There was no mark on him, but his eyes were wide open, staring, and there was an expression of unbelievable horror on his face.

Chapter Thirteen

For an instant I just stood there, paralyzed. Then a cold, hard rationality took over.

I should check to make sure he was dead. I stared, focusing hard through the darkness and my daze. There was no sign of breathing. Pulse? I couldn't, I simply couldn't, touch that body.

Then I must get help. That was it. I must go for help. The paralysis broke, and my feet moved like a sleepwalker's. Turn. Start down the path toward home. Bonne Espérance, that was home now. Walk carefully, watch for the swamp. Watch out for snakes and worse. Don't run; that would be too dangerous. Don't scream.

I held onto every scrap of sanity and control as I made my way doggedly. It was deep dark now. I had lost all sense of time. Past the fork in the road. That was familiar. Past a fallen tree branch I remembered. *Where was Mark? Why wasn't Mark here? Mark would come, not the dark-frowning, belligerent Mark, but the Mark I loved. Dear God, please send Mark. Then every-*

thing will be all right. There wasn't any body. There couldn't be a body. It was all my imagination . . . or something in the tea. . . .

A hysterical laugh rose to my lips. And then it died.

Something was with me, and it was not Mark. That "presence" again, somehow warning me? The one Amalic had said was coming to me because of my "gifts"?

All the while my feet kept moving. My eyes stayed on the path, looking neither left nor right. Something inside me kept me going.

And then, out of the swamp and darkness, something came. I didn't see nor hear it. I didn't sense it coming. Suddenly it just was *there*, touching my legs as if a ghostly hand had reached from the swamp and grabbed me. And I screamed.

I screamed, and I ran—blunderingly, senselessly. The presence, whatever it was, must have been guarding me, because I did not fall. Then, just as tongues of fire shot through my legs and heaving lungs, arms grabbed me.

Not ghostly arms out of a swamp—human arms, and all too strong. They grabbed and held me. I kicked and fought, and then through my panic and my screams a voice reached me.

"Tracy! Tracy, what's wrong? It's me!"

It was my father! I twisted to throw my arms around him, sobbing.

It was minutes before I could speak coherently. As soon as I could I blurted out, "Body . . . back there . . . by the swamp!"

I'll always be grateful that he took me seriously. We hadn't seen each other for years—we hardly knew each other—and I blurted out this unbelievable thing, and he believed me. Dad said, very quietly and calmly,

"Hang on to me, Tracy. Breathe slow and deep; that's it. Now, where was it?"

"Back . . . back there." I pointed.

"Right." Dad slid an arm around my waist. With his other hand he produced a flashlight. "I should have had this on earlier; I wouldn't have scared you. I grabbed it when I heard Shadow shriek. When he raced home without you, I didn't wait to put it on. There was moonlight enough to see by till I got deep in the bush. Then I heard you scream, and I didn't stop for anything. Now, do you think you can show me where the body is?"

He was so calm and collected that for the first time I could believe in the Ken Fairbrother Catriona had described, the man whom the government had sent into trouble spots and danger zones. Who could be writing a book so revealing that people and powers would want to scare him off or shut him up.

We passed the fork in the road and kept on going. I swallowed hard. "It should be right up there. I remember that clump of camellias right after I left . . . *it*." They were ghostly in the darkness. We went round the bend, and I stopped.

"That's funny," I said stupidly.

Dad ran the beam of the flash across the path. There was nothing there.

"The body must be farther on. Time gets disjointed when you're in shock." Dad strode ahead of me, throwing the beam of light from side to side. Its rays touched the roses foaming against the ruined cottage, and I gasped. "What?" Dad asked sharply.

"We *must* have passed it. It was after I left here."

Dad gave me a searching glance, then went through and around the cottage. "Nothing there. That's the original Dulaine cottage; Catriona doesn't let people come here because the floor's not safe. Nothing's been disturbed and no one's fallen through. You must have confused the time sequence."

We turned back, and with the powerful flashlight surveyed every inch, not just of the path, but of the swamps beyond, between the cottage and where Dad had found me. At last Dad stopped and looked at me ruefully. "I'm sorry."

"You don't believe me," I said dully.

"I believe your eyes saw what you said you saw. What that was is open to interpretation." He took me through the whole scene again, point by point, then shook his head. "You may have seen someone sleeping off a drunk, and only thought he wasn't breathing. It was dark. Your eyes may have been playing tricks on you. Where did you say you'd been?"

I hadn't. I waved my arm vaguely. "Over there somewhere. I had tea with—with the herb lady." Just in time I remembered my promise of silence to Amalie. I couldn't have said much more anyway; now that the shocks had worn off I was giddy again and very, very tired. I clutched at my father's arm as the world seemed to go around.

"Come on," my father said firmly, "we're going home. Any more of a search can wait for daylight."

Catriona was waiting for us. She took one look and ordered me to bed. "And leave a night-light on so you won't be seeing ghosts!"

"Not seeing, *feeling*," I corrected weakly.

"She's been drinking herb tea with one of your tenants," Dad told Catriona, who at once became alert.

"What was it? Lemon flavor? That could be balm, or thyme, but you don't know *what* else was in it. *Tansy* cakes? Tansy in large doses could definitely make you loopy! The islanders have built up a tolerance, judging from Zipporah, but you haven't. Stay away from island kitchens till you recognize what you're eating and how the unfamiliar ingredients may affect you!"

I was too tired to protest as she marshaled me to bed. Soon afterward Dad joined us, bearing a laden tray.

"We've been holding dinner, waiting for you to show up." He dished steaming shrimp jambalaya into three plates. The jambalaya was very spicy. I choked and sputtered and reached hastily for iced tea, and Dad and Catriona laughed.

We laughed a lot, during that impromptu feast, me in bed, Catriona in the slipper chair, and Dad on the love seat. It felt so strange. I hadn't seen my father for—what was it, three years? In those years, I'd grown up, and my father seemed to have gotten younger. The dark auburn hair like mine was now worn a bit longer, and he had a slight beard. In that moment of terror when I'd clung to him, we'd reestablished the father-daughter bond; now we were establishing a bond as friends. And as a new family. When Dad handed Catriona her plate, he gave her a casual, married-people hug, and it seemed natural and right. Dad-Mom-and-me was long over; Dad-Catriona-and-me had begun, and it was okay. I belonged.

"Where's Mark?" I finally thought to ask, and Catriona grimaced.

"He didn't show up either. And the boat's gone. Your father had to get someone else to run him over from the mainland. I'm going to tear a few strips off that cousin of mine tomorrow!"

But she didn't, because Mark wasn't there. He was gone, the *Silver Cat* was gone, and rain poured from a leaden sky. Some time in the middle of the day the *Silver Cat* reappeared at its moorings, but Mark did not. I knew that because my father came back from searching the path to the cottage and reported that he'd gone down to the dock and seen the boat.

Dad had conducted this search alone, and that made me even more certain that there was some truth in Mark's comments: My father had things he wished to hide. Dangerous things. The tautness in Dad's face when he came in to report his fruitless search reinforced this, and so did the way he shut himself in the library with the doors closed for the rest of the day. Today, in the grim gray light, there were dark currents underlying the warm sense of family I'd felt the night before.

Those currents made me shiver whenever I thought of my experience in the swamp, and I thought of it more often than I admitted. Okay, maybe I *had* imagined that whoever I'd seen was dead, but I had seen someone. So where had he gone to?

Teatime came, and Catriona disappeared from the study where we'd been working. She returned with a loaded silver tray. "This is a good day for tea. Light the fire, will you, Tracy?" She went to the library door and knocked firmly for my father.

We had a drawn-out, cozy time, and the sense of dark currents faded. That warm sense of our having become a family grew stronger as the three of us went to the kitchen and foraged for our dinner. Zipporah was feeling sick again, Catriona said. We had a good time cooking by ourselves, and afterward we ate the results at the big kitchen table. Mark did not appear, but late in the night I heard floorboards creak overhead. Mark must be back, and prowling through the old governess's room.

I wanted him. I wanted him terribly; wanted him

to put his arms about me and hold me so tight, I could not breathe. I needed him as I had needed him when I was in the swamp—to find me and hold me and make me safe. But this time he did not come to me. And if he *was* upstairs, I did not go to see.

Chapter Fourteen

That night, again, I awoke to feel a presence in my room, and when I put on the light, there was no one there. The French door, half ajar, was rattling in a wet breeze and the gauze curtains clung damply to the panes. The floor around the window was wet. I shut the window and locked it, but I didn't feel the love seat's cushion for possible warmth. The presence, rather than frightening me, had been oddly reassuring. As if it had come to tell me I had not been going crazy, or freaking out on herb tea, when I saw the body. I went back to bed.

The rain was gone by morning, but the sky was an odd yellow-gray. At breakfast everything was, on the surface, normal. Zipporah, shuffling as though her legs hurt her, brought in grits and eggs with a portentous frown. When I said politely that I hoped she was better, she gave me one of her inscrutable looks.

"Mmm-hmm. Cat be walkin'." She left the room before Catriona could catch her eye.

Dad and Catriona exchanged glances. "If I didn't know she was flat on her back last evening, I'd swear Zipporah had heard about Tracy's experience in the swamp," Dad said.

"What experience?"

Mark. His voice made me jump. He had come silently, on sneakered feet, through one of the open balcony doors.

"Tracy thinks she saw a body on the path to the old cottage," Catriona said.

Mark started. "That's crazy!" he said sharply. He swung toward me. "I thought you knew better by now than go prowling beyond the dig!"

The aggressiveness in his tone wiped out all my longing for his comfort. "I wouldn't have, if you'd shown up yesterday when you said you would," I retorted, and turned to Catriona. "Do you have some work for me to do in the house today? With you?"

I put the slightest emphasis on that last word, and Catriona, her face carefully unexpressive, said she was sure she did. Blessedly she didn't ask why Mark and I were on the outs, not then nor later. We worked side by side in the study, while Zipporah sang mournful spirituals in the kitchen.

"She's really low. I don't think she's well. Tracy, don't tell her more than you need to about last night," Catriona said in a low voice. "It would be all she needed to convince her for sure the Cat was walking."

"I won't." But I was convinced that, in some mysterious way, Zipporah already knew all about it.

Dad had gone out, and I thought Mark had too. Neither of them showed up for lunch, which Catriona and I ate beneath a slowly revolving ceiling fan on the gallery. The sky remained strange, and the air was still and clammy.

"When I was little, and had been listening to Zipporah's stories, I used to think spirits were waiting out there beyond the bushes on days like this," Catriona said softly.

I shivered.

"I think I'll go stretch my legs," I said, deliberately cheerful. I went down the outer stairs. As I stepped down from the last iron tread Mark materialized from the shadows beneath the gallery.

I must have jumped, or flinched. "I didn't mean to scare you," Mark said swiftly. He glanced upward in the direction of Catriona. "Look, can we talk a minute?" He led the way into the shadows and stood close by me, not touching, bracing himself by one arm against the wall.

"I just wanted to say I'm sorry about yesterday."

"Sorry for what? Standing me up? Or saying I was crazy?"

Mark drew his breath. "Okay, I shouldn't have said that. I wanted to let you know I couldn't meet you, honest. Something came up."

"Job?"

"Kind of." Mark's eyes, red-rimmed and strained, avoided mine. "Look, I just can't tell you about it now, okay? And I'd appreciate it if you wouldn't go into the subject with them." He pointed upward. "Cat would only worry for nothing. She tends to be a mother hen, as you'll find out."

"Something's wrong, isn't it?"

"No! It was just a job I had to do, with some guys she doesn't like. Everything's okay now." A slow smile slid across Mark's face. "So long as you don't go trying to convince people you saw imaginary bodies!"

"I wasn't imagining—!" I blushed. "Okay, maybe I'd been drinking too much herb tea."

Mark pounced on that, and I answered vaguely that I'd been visiting one of the island's herb women. "Tracy, don't *do* dumb things like that! You have no idea what's in that herb stuff. Don't go there again!"

"Okay, okay," I mumbled.

Mark looked at me. "Maybe you really *did* see something, but it must have been an alligator sleeping across the path."

I started to say I knew the difference between an alligator and a man, then decided I'd rather look as if the suggestion was too silly for me to answer.

"What did your father say about what you saw?" Mark asked suddenly.

"What? Oh . . . that it must have been my unconscious playing tricks. From hearing too many island legends, or the tea."

"Oh," Mark said. He seemed tense; he held his body unnaturally straight, as if he were deliberately avoiding touching me. I went back upstairs with the uneasy comfort of believing that Mark's body had been tense with something that had nothing to do with me.

Catriona and I worked late into the afternoon. This time it was my father who interrupted us with iced tea. We had it in the air-conditioned library. Mark came and joined us, and when we had finished off the pitcher of tea, he lingered, as if in need of some kind of community.

Dad put a Debussy record on the stereo. Catriona suggested that he read aloud to us; apparently that was one of their favorite ways to relax. Dad chose a poem.

I'd never known that reading aloud was one of my father's talents. The poem was *The Marshes of Glynn*, and it made me think of the island, and of my lonely walk last night. Outside the gray sky began to dim and blur into the darker shadows of the live oaks with their veils of moss. In the kitchen the odors of seafood and okra began to rise, and Zipporah hummed her blues-sounding hymns. Somewhere, out beyond the camellias, a peacock screamed.

Close at hand something crashed. Zipporah cried out. We all jumped up, and as we did the door from the hall swung open. Zipporah stood there, her right hand wrapped in her apron and her face bleached gray.

"Miss Cat, I done drop your grandma's cut-glass pitcher. Dinner on de stove. I got to go. De Silver Cat done tell true true."

"Never mind dinner or the pitcher," Catriona said swiftly. "Zipporah, dear, what's happened? Leave the Cat out of it, just tell me."

"Cat be walkin', like I told you. My grandson Cuffy, he be dead. Sophra just be here to tell me." Zipporah closed her eyes. Her voice became markedly more singsong and more Gullah. "Cuffy, he good chile, but longtime now he go wrong wrong, not fear de Lord. He be out fishin' in de swamp last night, an' he fall an' drown. An' de smell of dat cheap beer he drink be on him."

"Oh, Zipporah," Catriona whispered with compassion. She put her arms quickly around the old housekeeper. Dad stepped forward, looking sympathetic but unsure what to do. Mark—

Cuffy was Mark's friend, Catriona had said so. I turned around quickly.

Mark was leaning against the wall, staring across—not at me; at the portrait of St. Pierre above the fireplace. His body was no longer tense and stiff. His eyes were wet. I remember thinking, irrelevantly, that he'd hate my seeing that.

I remember more that the look in his eyes was not just grief but something strangely like relief.

Chapter Fifteen

The look lasted only a moment. Then Mark said curtly, "No reason for Zipporah to walk across the island. I'll hitch up Shadow." He disappeared out the window. Zipporah just stood there, her eyes unseeing, swaying slightly to the faint "Mmm-mmmm" she was crooning.

Catriona turned her gently toward the door. "Come on, honey. You'll want to change. I'll help you." They went downstairs to Zipporah's room.

I stood there feeling helpless. My father gave me a wry half smile and touched my shoulder. "Leave them be. Mark too," he added. "We're not islanders. Catriona will know how to cope."

"At least I can finish cooking dinner," I said, and went into the kitchen. My father followed. From the kitchen window we could see Mark drive off with a black-clothed Zipporah. Presently Catriona came back and sat down at the kitchen table to watch our efforts. "You didn't go," I said, half a question. Catriona shook her head.

"Zipporah will be planning the—death ceremonies. She won't want me there, listening to it all
like an archaeologist, not a mourner. I couldn't abide
Cuffy, even when he was little, and she knows it.
Mark, on the other hand, used to be practically his
blood brother, and apparently still is—was," she corrected. "At least he kept defending him whenever—
No matter. Mark will either be a big help over there,
or he'll clear out. Whatever, we probably won't see
him again till the services are over."

She rose with effort and began setting the kitchen
table.

Catriona was wrong about our not seeing Mark
for days. I couldn't sleep that night. Or rather, I slept
and waked, and sometime around two in the morning
the still pressure that had been building in the sky all
day broke with a crash of thunder. Lightning flashed,
and then a gust of wind sent the French doors rattling,
and rain came down in torrents.

In my bare feet and nightshirt I ran to shut the
windows before the old French rug was soaked. The
wind was making the rain come at a terrible slant, and
water bounced off the gallery flooring and ran inside.
Were the windows downstairs closed? Zipporah usually did that if it were needed. I opened my bedroom
door to check the master bedroom, then remembered
that it had new carpeting—no antique rugs to ruin. I
closed the drawing-room windows and then ran downstairs, flicking on light switches as I did so.

Everything was open except the front door. I raced
around the rooms, slamming rattling windows and
throwing the heavy brass levers that locked them to
the floor. *Il faut ne réveiller pas le Chat d'Argent.*
Zipporah had said the Silver Cat was walking, and
that it brought death and danger in its wake. There

had already been dangers—the crashing chandelier; my fall in the swamp, and from Shadow. Catastrophes always came in threes. *Cat*-astrophes. I was getting slaphappy or something. What did I think I was doing? Locking death out? You couldn't lock out death, or spirits.

Zipporah was probably sitting up somewhere, praying with Sister Janie and other islanders for Cuffy's spirit. I'd read somewhere, in Catriona's papers, that the islanders believed the spirits of people who died violent deaths could not rest in peace. Drowning in the swamp had been violent—or had Cuffy been too drunk to know what was happening?

Had he been alone?

It was at that point that I began to feel a prickle up my spine. And then it vanished, wiped out by something that mattered more. Above the splash of rain I heard the sound of wagon wheels in gravel. I was in the study. I ran out to the gallery and saw Mark unhitching Shadow. The stallion's gray coat glimmered through the blackness as Mark led him to his pasture. I sat down in a rocker on the gallery and waited.

After a while I sensed Mark coming up the back steps. I didn't make a sound, but when he reached the gallery, he stopped. The light from the study fell across him. He was soaking wet, his clothes and hair plastered against him. He looked like a drowned panther.

For a minute he just stood there, drenched and weary. Then he started toward me slowly.

I rose, wordlessly, and held out my arms. Wordlessly Mark came into them. His arms went around me, holding me so tight, I could hardly breathe. I could feel the pounding of his heart, and his heaving sobs. I sat back down in the rocker, drawing Mark down with me. He was on his knees, his head buried against my chest and then my lap, and I cradled him there as if he were a child.

We were reliving that scene by the swamp, only with roles reversed. This time I was the stronger. For these minutes we were one.

After a while Mark straightened, taking a deep breath. "Sorry."

"You don't have to apologize. Is Zipporah all right?"

"Zipporah," Mark said, "is in total command of the situation as usual. Even when she's half in a trance, which is what I'd have found myself in if I'd stayed much longer. The singing and the shouting were getting to me."

"Shouting?"

"Crooning and praying and dialogue, all mixed together. This is no time to go into cultural differences." Mark looked at me and started to laugh. "We must be some pair. You look like a waif lost in the storm."

"What do you think you look like?" I took the sleeve of my nightshirt and dried his face. "Have you had anything to eat?"

"Too much. The islanders believe mourning and eating go together. Is there any coffee left in the pot?"

"I'll make some." We went into the kitchen, arms around each other. Mark took off his wet shirt and draped it over a kitchen chair. I made coffee, black and bitter as I knew by now he liked it. I made myself tea. We sat at the table, making the kind of small talk people do after a death has occurred. Not touching.

I asked if anyone knew what had caused Cuffy's accident, and Mark said emphatically that it was because Cuffy'd been out in the swamps while drinking.

"The guy always was a fool about things like that. Reckless. He felt he knew the island like his own hand, and he was smart smart, and nothing could ever happen to him, no matter what." He took a deep gulp of coffee and pushed the mug toward me for a refill with a grateful look.

"You really loved him, didn't you?" I asked softly, pouring.

"We were like brothers. We always knew we could count on the other to look after us. Or cover up for us."

"Cover up?"

Mark shrugged. "Heck, we were always in trouble, one or both of us, when we were kids. Never anything as bad as my grandparents used to think. We understood each other."

He was using the past tense, and I couldn't tell whether it was because he'd adapted already to Cuffy's being dead, or because the situation had changed before that. "Too bad you weren't out fishing with Cuffy the night it happened," I said tentatively, and then wished I hadn't. Mark's face darkened.

"Yeah. Well, I wasn't." He gave a bitter laugh. "Maybe his time had come, the way folks were saying. Or else it was the curse of the Silver Cat that did him in."

"Is *that* what they think?"

"Sure. What did you expect? Cuffy was trying to get away from the island and island ways. Make something of himself, one way or another. Maybe with his music. But the island got him. Or the island curse."

"Does Zipporah believe that?" I demanded, shocked.

"You'll have to ask her." Mark rose. "Thanks for the coffee and—everything. I'm going to sack out." He kissed me, gently, and went up the outside stairs to his room. I turned out the lights and made my way up the circular staircase, deeply shaken.

I didn't tell Dad or Catriona about any of this.

The next day the sun was white-hot. There was no wind, and the Spanish moss hung limply, but the marshes sighed and whispered as if from an invisible breeze. Zipporah was still not there. Mark wasn't either. "He went out in the *Silver Cat* right after dawn," Dad said, seeing me look toward Mark's empty place at the breakfast table.

"How was he?" I asked guardedly.

"I didn't get to speak to him. He took the *Cat* out of the harbor like a bat out of hell."

In midmorning Catriona packed a suitcase for Zipporah and drove it over to the settlement on the far side of the island. Dad and I worked for a while, he in the library, I in the study. All at once he pushed back his chair and ran down to the cellars. He reappeared in the backyard with a ladder, rope, and two heavy bells.

"What are you doing?" I demanded from the gallery.

"Rehanging the warning bells. Catriona showed them to me a couple of months ago. The small one's for calling Bonne Espérance people back to the house. We'll have to work out a code. The big one's the island's traditional trouble signal. It means 'Everybody come.' If these had been up the other night, we could have rung them when we first started worrying about you."

I helped him hang them from weathered iron hooks in two of the live oak trees.

Catriona came back, looking troubled. "I knew this would happen. Mr. Rafiel Jones is already weaving a story around Cuffy's death. They're chanting it at the shouting. Cuffy's body was scratched up from being in the water, and somebody started saying it was the mark of the Cat. That he didn't die naturally. As if passing out drunk wasn't natural for him!"

Was I imagining things, or was there a trace of uneasy doubt beneath Catriona's words? I glanced at her sharply.

"Cuffy always was a wrong 'un," Catriona added. I was glad Mark wasn't there to hear her.

After lunch, without need for discussion, Catriona and I gravitated to the dig and worked for several hours until Dad's ringing of the small bell called us home. He had spent most of the afternoon on the phone with his publisher, something about the need for security clearances for portions of his manuscript. Otherwise the publisher was afraid of a government lawsuit. The conversation between Dad and Catriona about this, during dinner, was mostly over my head, but it set me thinking.

"Did you tell Dad about the chandelier falling?" I asked suddenly.

Both my father and Catriona stared at me, his face alarmed and hers unreadable. *"What?"* Dad demanded, and I told him.

"Ken, don't worry! The chandelier can be fixed, and my leg is fine now," Catriona said hastily. "It wasn't anything you did wrong when you ran the new cable. The hardware store probably didn't sell you heavy enough steel, that's all. So it broke when the old cable broke. It's no big deal."

"Yes, it is. The cable was cut halfway through."

I hadn't known I was going to say that till I did. There was a shocked stillness, not just from Dad and Catriona, but from Mark, who had just pulled one of his as-if-by-magic reappearances. "Ask Mark," I added. "He saw it too. I know he did."

"She's right," Mark said curtly as Catriona paled. "Somebody's trying to get rid of somebody." He turned to my father. "Zipporah's right. You'd better think about getting the three of you and your book-writing off the island. Before you wake any more sleeping cats!"

I stared at Mark, my mind a tumult. *He wanted us to go. No, he didn't, he was afraid for us. He couldn't believe the curse was behind Cuffy's death—or could he?* As if he'd read my mind, Mark said, "There's more than one kind of sleeping cat," and looked straight at my father.

Meaning again that Dad's work was a danger to us. And that Cuffy's death was in some way connected? My skin prickled.

"We're letting ourselves get carried away," Dad said after a silence, very quietly. "My book's no more a danger to us than St. Pierre's curse is. Let's finish dinner, and then let's all go up to our sitting room and watch TV. There's a good movie on."

"Just so it's not a horror film," Catriona said.

She was joking, but I realized that she wasn't denying the connections between Cuffy's death and the falling chandelier with either Dad's book or with the curse.

Chapter Sixteen

That night I dreamed about my ride home through the swamp. I watched it all in slow motion—the eeriness of the lonely path, the white-glimmering moss, and Shadow rearing. The sound of his shriek, and the thud of his hooves as he galloped off. And me, picking myself up, going searching. I saw the body, but not in the dark—as if the beam of Dad's flashlight were thrown full on it. I saw the face, and it was the face of the man under the Savannah streetlight, horribly distorted. It had looked on hell, and across the face and throat were deep, dark-red slashes: the clawmarks of an enormous cat.

I woke sitting straight up in bed, wet with perspiration, and my heart was pounding. And then it came, as slowly as fog rolling in, that sense that I was being visited by an entity, a presence. Come now not to warn, but to reassure. I bolted upright, my fingers digging into the mattress on either side. My skin was crawling even as the pounding in my chest grew still.

The presence grew stronger. I heard and felt nothing, but I knew something was moving from the French door to my bed. And leaping up. . . .

Something small and compact and very feminine settled itself against my feet and began to purr.

My left hand was able to move again. It reached out cautiously and felt for the bedside lamp, then switched it on.

Folded up comfortably near the foot of my bed, feet tucked beneath her neatly, was a small silver-colored Persian cat. Her purr was going rhythmically, and she gazed at me with enormous sapphire eyes.

I laughed aloud, and as if that were an invitation, the little cat crept forward and curled up in my lap. She was no ghost. She was warm and very real, and her back arched in ecstasy as I scratched it.

"Are *you* the ghost who visited me that night?" I asked, relieved. She blinked sleepily. It made sense. It definitely made sense. My window was always open, and the little cat obviously knew her way around my room. The love seat must have been warm because she'd been sleeping there. She probably thought the room belonged to her, not me. She'd probably been sleeping here for months—*Mark* had been able to get in and out, to make himself at home, before Dad and Catriona moved in. But she was no stray—her fur was too well kept, and she wore a collar of braided blue satin ribbon.

"You probably have somebody on the island worried sick when you disappear at nights," I scolded, and she blinked sleepily and snuggled up next to me.

I put the light out and went to sleep again myself, and when I woke to daylight, the little cat was gone.

"I've had a roommate," I announced as soon as I went down to breakfast, and related the account of my earlier visitor. "But it wasn't the Dulaine Silver Cat, it was a real one," I finished triumphantly, and described my night, omitting the bit about the nightmare.

Catriona looked puzzled. "I've seen a lot of cats around the island, but I can't remember any pale-gray Persian."

"If there's a cat like that wandering around the island at night," Dad said, "it could explain where all this talk about the Silver Cat walking is coming from."

"She's not a wild cat. She's somebody's pet. She wears a collar."

"Ask Zipporah," Dad suggested.

"A silver cat's the last thing Zipporah needs to hear about the day of Cuffy's funeral," Catriona said. "Anyway, she isn't here. But you could ask Mark." I nodded vaguely.

I didn't know where I stood with Mark. Watching TV together last night in the upstairs sitting room, with Dad and Catriona present, had been unnerving. We'd sat on the couch together, Mark and I, side by side but not touching. He had been, to say the least, uncommunicative, but across the small deep gulf between us I could feel his tension. It could be he was embarrassed because I'd seen him cry, but I had a feeling it was much, much more. Not just Cuffy's dying either.

Mark hadn't wanted anyone to know about the cut chandelier cable, but he'd backed me up when I told. The attraction between us was very, very strong, but Mark thought that I, that all of us, should leave the island. Mark thought my father was waking a sleeping cat of danger.

Catriona was right. I had to talk to Mark.

But there wasn't a chance, because he wasn't in the house now. I knew, because I'd searched it, room by room. His bedroom door was locked, and he didn't answer my repeated knocks.

I went back downstairs to see if I could do some work for Catriona. "She's gone to be with Zipporah for Cuffy's death rites," my father said.

"I thought the funeral wasn't till this afternoon!" I exclaimed, startled.

"It isn't. Apparently there's a custom of friends and family keeping watch by the corpse. Especially in cases of unnatural death."

Unnatural death.

"You can do some work for me if you want to keep busy," Dad said, seeing me change color. So I worked with him in the library, fetching notes out of the files for him and filing others.

I was jamming a folder into a crowded file drawer when I saw the title of the file beyond it. *Entrance, Means of Effecting*. I took it out, curious.

Inside the file were a jumble of clippings, hand-written notes, and memos detailing how to enter fortified or barricaded buildings . . . how to blow the lock off a safe without destroying it . . . how to pick locks. A part of my mind registered with stupefaction that there certainly were a lot of things I didn't know about my father. The other part, the main part, looked at the Xeroxed instructions on how to pick old door-locks.

"Excuse me," I said in an unnatural voice. I stuck the Xerox in my pocket and went upstairs to the school-room-nursery, where there was an old hat on a rack with a hatpin and old-fashioned, heavy hairpins in it.

I took the hatpin, and the hairpins, and I picked Mark's lock.

It didn't happen as fast as I make it sound, and

I didn't know exactly what I had in mind. Maybe that Mark was inside, and there was something wrong. Whatever, the door swung open finally onto an empty room. I went inside and, quite deliberately, looked around.

Mark's room was like him—surprising. Two walls were tangerine, and two were black. An inexpensive shag rug, black and white, lay on the floor. The bed, pushed against the wall, was covered with a black sheepskin, and there were big toss pillows—black, white, tangerine, and scarlet. An old bureau and one of the armoires that at Bonne Espérance stood in for closets. Cement block–and–board bookcases, and a board-topped file-cabinet desk, that looked as if Mark had rigged them up himself. On the walls a rock poster and a poster of last year's Savannah jazz festival.

And a snapshot. I didn't have to get close to recognize it. It was a picture of me I'd sent to Dad and Catriona when I wrote asking permission to come live with them.

All at once I felt weak. I sat down on the bed, in the process knocking two magazines to the floor. I bent to retrieve them, and my fingers encountered something small and hard. A small glass vase, oddly shaped, with two spoutlike openings. Rather like the priceless old Chinese Export tulipière vase Catriona had in the master bedroom, only that one had five spouts for flower stems instead of two, and was made of china, not glass. I started to put the glass vase on the bureau, then realized this was not a good idea. Mark would be furious if he discovered I'd been in here, and I could hardly blame him. Anyway, I hadn't discovered anything that would explain why he was so—haunted.

I returned the vase to the floor beneath the edge

of the sheepskin, put the magazines back on top, and got out of there, managing finally to lock the door behind me. Then, still feeling ashamed of myself, I went into the nursery to return the tools of my crime.

I just happened to glance out the window, and there was Mark, heading purposefully across the yard to vanish into the maze of ground-level storage rooms.

Without stopping to lose my nerve, I ran downstairs. Mark wasn't there. The door to the cellar was just ajar. I helped it open farther, and from somewhere down below me I heard a voice. Not Mark's. Zipporah's.

Zipporah was there, on the day of Cuffy's funeral, while the deathwatch was still going on. She wasn't crying or keening, she wasn't talking about spirits or silver cats. She was speaking in cold level anger, and she was speaking to Mark.

"Boy, you hear me, and you hear me good. I hold my peace till Cuffy be buried, that be only right and proper. He de son of my son, and I want no shame to his name. But after de sun sink on his burying, I'll not let another sun go down without I speak de truth. It be no spirit struck Cuffy down, and it be no strong drink."

"But, Zipporah—" That was Mark's voice. Zipporah cut in swiftly.

"Don't you 'But, Zipporah' me! I be going to name Cuffy's death for what it be. *Murder*. Less'n I speak de truth, my grandson's spirit not sleep. I won't wait till there be more deaths on my conscience. You want more chandeliers to fall?"

There was a deadly silence. Then Zipporah said gruffly, "I know you grievin'. I know you tied. But, boy, you cut loose now or you be hurt bad bad."

And then, breaking the tension like comic relief

in tragedy, came Catriona's voice, upstairs somewhere. "Ken, darling! Are you still planning to attend the funeral with me? Because I've got to be driving Zipporah back there right away!"

Zipporah's heavy footsteps moved toward the cellar stairs. Like the wind I had the cellar door closed. I was running barefoot, my sandals in my hand, up the stairs to the main floor. I was calling out to Catriona, "Wait till I change my clothes fast. I want to go too!" and running to my room.

I was down in the carriage, in a proper navy linen dress and heels, before Zipporah appeared in a black dress and big-brimmed hat and heavy veil. She was monumental, like a queen out of Greek tragedy grieving for her children.

We rode to the funeral in absolute silence.

I didn't know what I'd been expecting at an island funeral, but it was all of those things and more. It was held in a small chapel built of tabby. There was black fabric like veiling draped over the chapel's blue door. Blue to hold off ghosts. Inside, despite open windows, the heat was intense. Sister Janie Ruth Ford, in a white minister's robe, stood in the pulpit. The pews were packed—men in clean, carefully ironed workclothes or pressed dark suits, women in cotton housedresses or Sunday best. Most wore hats. Many held flowers. There were flowers everywhere, their scent cloyingly sweet and suffocating.

Zipporah was conducted by two elderly ushers to the chief mourners' pew, marked with black ribbons and white flowers. Dad and Catriona and I were shown seats near the center—in deference, probably, to Zipporah's close ties with Catriona's family.

"Let us call upon the Lord," Sister Janie Ruth said.

There were prayers, from the pulpit and from the pews. There were testimonies to God's wisdom and comfort, and to Cuffy's good intentions. Nobody, I noticed, said anything about Cuffy being good. There were Scripture readings and eulogies by both Sister Janie Ruth and Mr. Rafiel Jones, all interrupted in soft affirmation by murmurs of "Yes, Lord" and "That be true, Lord" from the pews.

There was singing, and there was the "shouting" Mark had spoken of—strange and alien to my eyes but beautiful, as feet moved in rhythmic shuffle and hands clapped together with spontaneous rhymed chanting. Then the congregation sat down again, and someone somewhere began to tap out a one-note tune with two crossed sticks, and someone else played a blues fiddle. The fiddle music, infinitely longing, ceased. The congregation stirred. A dignified middle-aged woman next to me tapped my arm and passed over three flowers, for Catriona and Dad and me.

Led by Zipporah, the people in the chief mourners' pew rose and filed by the open coffin, giving it their flowers. Row by row the other people followed. Now our row was rising. My legs felt wobbly and my stomach churned. I'd never seen a dead body, not unless you counted whatever that had been by the swamp. But I couldn't back out and disgrace Zipporah, not to mention Dad and Catriona. Already Dad was stepping out into the aisle, as naturally as if he'd been doing this kind of thing all his life. Maybe he had.

I wondered where Mark was. I wished he were beside me. I followed Catriona out into the aisle, and up it, staring at my shoes. When the foot of the coffin loomed into the periphery of my vision, I steeled myself to look up. And a claw tightened somewhere around my innards.

The body in the coffin, dressed in a heartbreakingly new black suit, was the body I'd tripped over on the path. It was the body of the handsome young black man who'd loitered under a Savannah streetlight. The eyes were closed now; there was no longer a look of unspeakable horror on the face. But the face was also no longer without a mark. From forehead to chin, even running across the eyelids, were slashes, as though he'd been raked by the claws of a giant cat.

Chapter Seventeen

Somehow I managed to lay my flower in the coffin. Somehow I managed to keep my face a mask. I tried not to look any longer at Cuffy's face, so dreadfully violated since his death. His hands were folded peacefully at his waist, purple-brown hands with nails bitten down like a child's, obediently folded.

I had to get out of there. I straightened, and as I did a magnetic pull came at me from across the room. Inexorably, unwillingly, my eyes met it.

Mark was standing there, over to one side with the pallbearers. He was in a dark suit I'd never seen, a flower in his buttonhole, and his dark eyes bored into mine. Threatening? Challenging? Pleading? I didn't know. I only knew I had to get away.

I shot Catriona an imploring glance, and I fled —down the aisle past our pew, and out into the yard.

The air was fresh here in the little clearing surrounded by pine barrens. Flowers bloomed, and over in the graveyard crosses and markers leaned, crooked with age, among tidy mounds littered neatly with bowls and coffeepots and farm tools, with shards of broken dishes. Broken pottery, symbolizing the brokenness of life, Catriona had explained. Cuffy's life had been broken young, and I could not explain it. I didn't believe that it had simply happened.

I didn't believe his death had been an accident, any more than it had been natural. Especially after what I'd heard Zipporah say.

I was going to be sick. I stumbled into the rim of the woods and leaned against a tree trunk, retching. Then I stumbled out again. My legs weren't cooperating enough to hold me up, certainly not enough to walk me home. I didn't want to be a part of Cuffy's burying. I knelt down a way off, in a field of wildflowers, and hugged myself to hold back the chill.

Singing still came from the church, but I heard no other sound. The shadow that came from behind me, looming over me, was soundless. Then Mark was kneeling behind me, rocking me in his arms. "Shhh, shhh. Just hang on. It's going to be all right."

A flash of anger gave me the strength to break away. I swung around. "Don't you *dare* tell me things will be all right! Not until you tell me what's all wrong!" Mark's mouth dropped open, but I rushed on. "No! Don't give me any more of your lies!"

Mark stared at me. "I don't know what you're talking about!"

"Of course, you do! You knew I saw that body, didn't you?" I persisted. "You knew it was Cuffy's. If you didn't know before, you knew when you looked at me across the coffin."

Mark didn't answer. His face had the look of the St. Pierre portrait. I caught my breath. "You *did* know before. That's why you were in such a foul mood till his body was found. And why you were relieved when

Zipporah finally heard and told us. You didn't trust me to understand. You kept on lying to me!"

Mark looked stricken, but he still didn't speak.

"You knew Cuffy was dead before everybody else did," I said shakily after a moment. "And you knew it wasn't drowning like they said. That's what's been eating you up so, isn't it? Keeping silent?" I walked away, hugging myself. "Why did you, Mark? Why are you letting these—stories about spirit retribution, or the curse of the cat, get started? You know Cuffy didn't drown. He wasn't in the water when I found him. You don't believe haunts got him, and neither does Zipporah!"

"Leave Zipporah out of this," Mark said tightly. "Hasn't she been hurt enough?"

"We've all been hurt, Mark! Catriona's your cousin, and I thought you loved her, but you kept quiet about that chandelier till I spoke out. I might have been killed, being thrown from Shadow, or in the swamp. Because somebody's been following me around the island."

That shook him, as nothing else so far had done. But he didn't question me. He shouted. "I told you not to go around the island alone, that it was dangerous—"

"Shut up!" I shouted back. "I was out alone that night because you'd stood me up that afternoon, remember?"

"I had to go in to Savannah to see—"

" '—to see a guy about a job.' I know!" I looked at him through bitter tears. "Are you sure you weren't lurking around the island somewhere so you could move Cuffy's body? *Somebody* did. Somebody knew Cuffy was dead. Why was the body moved, Mark? Why are you trying to get me to back off? Not just me—Dad, and Catriona. You keep telling me the island's dangerous for us, that we should go—*just for a while.* But you haven't told me why!"

"I can't," Mark said in anguish.

"Well, you'd better! What are you waiting for? Till one of us gets killed? Till you get killed? Because you're over your head in whatever's going on. I know it, Catriona knows it, Zipporah knows it. There's been one death already. The only way any of us will be safe is if you go public with what you know."

"I can't," Mark repeated doggedly. "Believe me."

"Give me one good reason I should believe a word you say."

A burst of music came from the church. The procession was coming out, led by the pallbearers carrying Cuffy's coffin.

"You've just got to trust me. We can't talk anymore."

Mark rose. So did I. "What did Zipporah mean when she said she wouldn't have any more deaths on her conscience?"

Mark drew his breath sharply and then shot a look toward the procession. "I'm supposed to be a pallbearer. I've got to go. Just keep your mouth shut!" He raced off across the field.

I went back to the carriage, and waited for Dad and Catriona. And I prayed. Hard.

A tumult of physical and emotional feelings were running wild in me, and gradually they all crystallized into one: *anger.*

It wasn't because I was being lied to, or patronized and shut out, or being made a fool of. It was because people I loved were in danger. I loved my father, and I loved Catriona, and their being here, writing their books here, was somehow dangerous. I loved Mark, and he was in anguish, and he couldn't tell me why.

Keep your mouth shut, Mark had said, and I knew I would, not because he told me to but because I needed to have more pieces of the puzzle before I'd be believed. *Keep out of it*, Mark had said, but I knew I couldn't. *Trust me*, he'd said, and I couldn't do that either. Not till I'd found out what the shadow was that lay over Dorr Island, and us all.

Chapter Eighteen

I knew what I had to do, but I didn't know how to do it. So I sat silent, and when Dad and Catriona came I rode back with them to Bonne Espérance. It was so quiet. A peacock strolled out of the forest and across the lawn, the closest to the house I'd ever seen one come.

Zipporah wasn't there. She had gone back to her daughter-in-law's house, Catriona said, and would return tomorrow. Catriona herself went to the kitchen, put the coffeepot on, and found some cream cheese and banana bread. I realized that we all were famished, that we hadn't eaten lunch.

We carried the tray into the library, and St. Pierre's portrait watched us as we ate. Catriona glanced up at the painting and shook her head. "Temperament can run in families, you know. A genetic predisposition. Extremes of mood, inability to control temper, or express emotion except in violence. . . ." She rubbed her hand across her eyes. "Forgive me. I'm rambling."

"No, you're not," I said. Dad rose from the sofa and crossed to the wing chair to kiss Catriona.

"You're a Dulaine. You control your temper, and your emotions find expression in love and kindness. Mark must have that as part of his heritage too."

"I wish I could believe that," Catriona said. "And I wish I knew where Mark is right now."

"I'll find him," I said. But when I'd changed into jeans and mounted Shadow bareback, I didn't go in search of Mark. I went wandering down the path past the deserted dig, and turned at the fork that had led me to Amalie's cottage.

She was gathering herbs in her garden, and she looked up and smiled without surprise. "Good afternoon, Tracy Fairbrother. I've been watching for you. The kettle is on, and there are muffins."

"Not tansy," I said apprehensively. Amalie gave an almost girlish giggle.

"No, sesame. Sister Janie Ruth Ford made them for the funeral meal, and kindly sent them."

"I thought you'd be at the funeral," I said.

Amalie shook her head. "Oh, my dear, no. I only go to happy occasions now. The only funeral I'll attend will be my own. I sent flowers though. Did you see them? Armfuls of bergamot and bluebells. And white daisies. White for funerals, and daisies for the young. The boy Cuffy was too young to die." She frowned, shaking her head faintly so the white curls danced in the sun.

"Amalie, why did he die?"

Amalie looked puzzled. "Ask Mark. Mark will know."

"Mark won't tell me, and I'm asking you. They were mixed up in something together, weren't they?

That's what you tried to warn me about. Just as Zipporah did."

"Poor Zipporah. Losing her grandson like this must have been a dreadful shock to her."

"Somehow I don't think it was. And I think you're trying to lead me off the subject, just as Mark does."

Amalie gave an apologetic little laugh. I took the bunch of herbs from her, then took her fragile hands and led her to the bench. "Please, Amalie. I need your help. You know the islanders, you probably know everything that goes on on Dorr Island. You told me to draw Mark into my world, but I don't know how."

"Oh, my dear, yes you do. You must use your strength. Love is always stronger than evil. You know that, Catriona." She had forgotten who I was, confusing me with my stepmother. But she knew whom we were talking about. "You must use your love to pull him from the swamp. Mark's a good boy. He's always been energized by love."

It was a strange choice of words, just as Amalie's speech was a strange mixture of the childlike and the profound. Or maybe they were two sides of the same coin.

We sat there in silence for a few minutes, while the late sun shone down a benediction. Then the herb borders rustled, and the little Gullah girl I'd seen before came toward us. She was followed by a small fluffy silver-colored cat.

I must have exclaimed aloud. The girl gave me a slantwise glance, and the cat twisted politely around my ankles. I reached down and patted her. "Isn't she beautiful? Is she yours?" I asked.

"She make home with Gran'Amalie," the girl murmured, and turned back to Amalie. "Please, ma'am, Gran'mammy sent me for tea. Her head hurt bad bad."

"Yes, of course." Amalie rose. "Miss Fairbrother,

this is Zipporah Bayne's granddaughter, Sophra. Make your curtsy like I've taught you, Sophra." Sophra bobbed. "And this little mischief is my Lucette."

Amalie darted into the cottage for a packet of tea, and the little cat followed her. Sophra went in too. I stood, watching the bees and butterflies grow intoxicated on flower nectar. And then, faint but unmistakable, I heard the sound of a music box. It was in the cottage, and it was playing "Clair de Lune."

As if hypnotized, I walked into the cottage. Sophra was standing in the center of the little parlor, gazing in enchantment at the old carousel music-box in Amalie's hands.

"Where did you get that?" I asked stiffly.

"Isn't it charming? My papa gave it to me when I was six. That's enough now, Sophra," Amalie said as the tune petered out. "Your grandmamma's waiting for her dose of tea. Run along. Come back in three days, and I'll give you whatever else she needs."

Sophra ran off into the woods. Amalie watched her from the doorway.

"That child knows more routes through the swamp than all the rest of us put together. If I didn't know her parents, Tracy, I'd think she were one of the island spirits."

At least she knew who I was again. I picked the little cat up and cuddled her. "Speaking of spirits, Amalie, your Lucette's scared me a couple of times. She's been waking me up, coming into my room. Only she's kept herself hidden, and all I knew was that *something* alive had been in the room with me."

Amalie looked alarmed. "She must have gotten into the habit of following Mark there, when he was living in the big house before Catriona and your father came. I hope she hasn't been a trouble."

I shook my head. "It's okay. And no, I won't tell Dad and Catriona whose cat she is. Though I do think Mark might have told me. Speaking of Mark—"

"We will speak no more of Mark until we've had our tea. Which shall we have today? Bergamot, I think."

It had been bergamot I'd laid in Cuffy's coffin. The memory rose sharply. "No tea. Please," I said thickly.

At the same moment Mark's voice spoke behind me. He had materialized once again out of nowhere. "Don't give Tracy herb tea, Gran'Amalie. Never. Promise me you won't. She's got allergies." Mark thrust his hand through my arm and said in his bossiest tone, "Come on."

"No. You won't talk to me, and I want to talk to Amalie."

"Not now. *We're* going to talk. But not here."

"Go. Go!" Amalie laughed, shooing us off with her fragile hands.

Mark marched me off and, before I could protest, lifted me bodily onto Shadow's back, then swung up behind me. One of his arms went round my waist; the other hand gripped Shadow's mane. He dug his heels into Shadow's sides.

"Where are we going?" I demanded as Shadow took off at a trot.

"Where we can talk in private. Which isn't back there, and isn't at Bonne Espérance. Those walls, as you darn well know, have ears. How the hell did you find out about Gran'Amalie, anyway? And what were you doing there?"

"I found her when I got lost one day," I said with dignity. "I went to have tea with her, and talk to her."

"Don't eat or drink anything there, do you hear me? You don't know—"

"I know she's the island herb doctor. And if Zipporah and Sister Janie Ruth respect her, that's good enough for me. I like her. And if it's any of your business, I wasn't going to eat or drink anything. I promised Dad." I felt Mark tense and added, "Don't worry, I didn't tell Dad and Catriona anything specific about Amalie. She asked me not to. I just said I'd been to visit the herb woman. Though Catriona must have known who that was. Amalie knows *her*."

"Catriona," Mark said, "hasn't been on the island for a long time. She doesn't know—" He stopped. "I really don't want to talk about it on the island. I asked your dad if I could take you to the mainland for dinner. Not on the waterfront. Somewhere quiet, and not fancy. You can come just the way you are."

"Okay."

"All *right*." Mark spurred Shadow to a gallop, and we tore past the big house and toward the dock. "Shadow can find his own way home," Mark said absently.

And then I felt him stiffen. Another speedboat was rocking beside the *Silver Cat* at the dock. As we slid down Shadow's back, a figure climbed ashore and started toward us. A dark-blond man in his late twenties, deeply tanned.

It was the man from the jazz club, the man who had threatened Mark at the boat that night. The man who had stared at me so hard. Not as if I'd been a prospective conquest. As if I'd been a slave on an auction block, whose usefulness—and expendability —he'd been appraising.

Chapter Nineteen

"What the hell are you doing here?" Mark demanded.

"Looking for you, kid. We have some unfinished business." The man was speaking to Mark, but he was looking at me. His eyes ran up me and then down again, slowly, and a slow smile spread across his face. "So this is the girl. Aren't you going to introduce me, partner?"

"This is Lon Estrada. A guy I used to hang out with around the docks when I was too young to know better," Mark said bluntly. He didn't mention my name. "Excuse us while we talk a few minutes? You go on aboard."

I obeyed, against my strongest impulse. Their conversation was very brief. Then Mark escorted Estrada back to his boat and stood there until he'd seen the other boat pull off.

When Mark rejoined me, his face was grim. "Don't ask," he said, forestalling comment. He slid into the

Silver Cat's pilot's seat, and I sat beside him, and we shot off into the sunset.

"We're not headed toward Savannah, are we?" I asked.

"I changed my mind. Anyway, I packed a basket for a picnic. Let's anchor off Fort McAllister and eat on board."

So that is what we did, eating bread and cheese and oysters and drinking soft drinks as the *Silver Cat* rocked gently and the glowing sunset faded into twilight. By unspoken consent we didn't speak of Dorr Island and its secrets till the last crumb was gone. Then, when Mark had lit the lamps and we'd moved to the inside cabin, I looked Mark squarely in the face.

"Okay, I'm waiting. Talk."

Mark looked at me helplessly. Then he rose, banging one fist into the other palm. "I don't know how to start!"

"Start with Cuffy. That *was* Cuffy's body I tripped over, wasn't it?" He nodded. "How did he die, Mark? Why was his body moved?"

"You heard how he died. He was drunk. Once too often, on that raw wood-alcohol he used to make. He learned how from his grandfather, who used to make the stuff during Prohibition, and he thought he was a big man, keeping it up," Mark said savagely. "Strictly illegal, of course. He used to sell it to drunks in town, and on the other islands. And to fool tourists who were looking for local color and thought they were being real hip to try it. Those idiots! That stuff could be poison, and Cuffy knew it."

"But Cuffy drank it," I said, not moving.

"Cuffy thought he was on top of things. So did I," Mark added almost to himself.

"Is *that* the 'bad bad' stuff you were involved in with Cuffy? Running moonshine?"

Mark looked almost relieved as he nodded.

"And that's what he died of? Drinking a bad batch of Zipporah's husband's 'recipe'?" I waited. "Mark, were you with him?"

"*No!* I told you, I was in Savannah seeing a guy." Estrada, I thought silently. I could definitely picture him mixed up with bootleg whiskey. "When I came back, I had to see Cuffy, so I went out looking for him. And," Mark said heavily, "I found him."

"It was you who moved the body, wasn't it? Mark, *why?*"

"Because," Mark said, "it would have killed Zipporah to find out that some of her husband's 'recipe' killed Cuffy. And he wasn't supposed to be that close to Bonne Espérance anyway. Your dad had warned him, after he pushed his way into the house one night. He was drunk and he owed some guys gambling money, so he was trying to get the money from Zipporah. Your father said if Cuffy came on our side of the island again, he'd call the police and report Cuffy's bootlegging." Mark smiled mirthlessly. "Catriona had ten fits when she found out I'd been running Cuffy and his product back and forth from the mainland on the *Silver Cat* after my old boat blew up."

I put two and two together and was appalled. "Is that what made your boat blow up? Bootleg liquor? Oh, Mark!"

"Don't you start," Mark said. "I've heard it all from Catriona."

"Why in heaven's name did you let yourself get mixed up with somebody who was such bad news?"

Mark made a wild gesture. "We were blood brothers when we were kids. When I showed up here, broke,

Cuffy staked me. He helped me revamp that old wooden hulk of a fishing boat, and got me my first charter customers. So when he wanted me to help him out, and paid me—" He shrugged. "We were *friends!*"

"And you paid back that friendship by making it look as though he'd been killed by the Dulaine curse?"

"I made it look as though he'd passed out drunk, which wouldn't have been the first time, and died by drowning, which has happened on these islands before. Okay," Mark said violently, "so I moved the body. I was trying to be kind. To protect somebody. Is that a crime? Tracy, I swear, I wouldn't have made his death look like something worse than it really was. I made it look like something less!"

"What about those scratches?"

"Maybe that happened while I was moving him." I didn't believe him, and it must have shown in my face. Mark came over and lifted me to stand facing him, very close. "I was making an accidental death look less incriminating. That's *all!* You've got to believe me."

"Zipporah said it was murder."

"Zipporah's wrong. I *know.* Nobody was responsible for Cuffy's death but Cuffy."

"How did the carousel music-box get in Amalie's cottage?"

The change of subject rocked Mark. He stared at me. And then he sat down, as if his legs had given out, the way mine had earlier in the graveyard. "Okay, I gave it to her. She loves presents, and I just wanted to do something nice for her. I had as much right to the music box as Catriona. Catriona wouldn't mind, if she knew."

"But she doesn't know. She doesn't know about Amalie at all, does she?" I walked away, frowning, trying to sort things out. "Amalie loves Catriona, but Catriona doesn't know about her. Cuffy died on the path to Amalie's cottage, and you moved his body far away. *Zipporah* knows Amalie, but she's never mentioned her name. And Amalie told me her father gave her the music box."

"Tracy, wake up! You know Amalie's half cracked. She's lost all conception of time," Mark said roughly. "Sometimes she thinks I'm St. Pierre! Sometimes she thinks she's our age! She told me about your coming to the cottage, only she said you were Catriona. You better believe I was pretty worried about that!"

"Why is it so important Catriona doesn't know she's there?" I caught at Mark's hands. "That's what's at the center of all this, isn't it? Mark, tell me."

"Okay," Mark said at last. "Okay. Only swear to God, I'd better be right to trust you." His face was pale. "Amalie is"—he swallowed hard. "She was my nurse when I was a kid. Hell, she practically raised me. Particularly after my folks died. Then she got old, and she got—peculiar. And my bloody hypocrites of grandparents railroaded her into a nursing home! They lied to her, they said they were sending her to a hotel for a holiday, and they committed her."

I made a faint shocked sound.

"I let my grandparents know what I thought about that," Mark said, looking at me hard. "And they didn't appreciate it. Next thing I knew, I was being packed off to a military school." He banged one hand into the other again. "I felt like such a louse. My grandparents had railroaded Amalie into a stinking old-age warehouse, and I hadn't stopped them."

"You weren't to blame for that. You were—how old, Mark?"

"Sixteen." Mark grimaced. "Military school taught me one thing—how to take care of myself. But I couldn't protect *her*. Not while my grandfather was around. He was too strong." He glanced at me briefly, then away. "You know about St. Pierre. Grandfather was like him in a way. Not the temper. The ruthlessness."

He stopped speaking for several minutes, and I waited. "Then I read in the papers about him dying, and about Natalie—she didn't like being called Grandmother, it made her feel too old—taking off for Europe. Natalie didn't give a damn about Amalie, so long as she didn't have to be around her. Then I finally graduated when I was eighteen," Mark said, "and I knew what I could do for Amalie. I—liberated her from the nursing home. Never mind how. And I brought her to Bonne Espérance."

"And then my father and Catriona came," I said after a pause.

Mark nodded. "I didn't dare trust Catriona. She had enough fits about my being there without permission, and my grandparents had filled her up with stories about what a sociopath I was. Anyway, I couldn't risk Amalie being sent back. I didn't have to worry about the islanders. They thought Amalie belonged here; they took care of her. It was your folks, and outsiders, that worried me."

"That's why you moved Cuffy. Not only to make things easier for Zipporah. So anybody who might investigate his death wouldn't find Amalie."

"I had to make sure nobody *did* investigate it," Mark said. "Cuffy would have understood. A guy does what he has to do. And you've got to let me do it, Tracy. You've got to promise to keep your mouth shut about all this."

"But Mark . . ." I paused. "It isn't right," I said at last, reluctantly. "For one thing Bonne Espérance belongs to Catriona, not to you."

"I'm a Dulaine too. Amalie's my responsibility."

"Maybe. But shouldn't she be Catriona's too? She'd help you, I'm sure she would, and Dad would too." I hesitated, groping for words. "Mark, this started out as a wonderfully kind thing, but it's gotten complicated. Can't you see that? It got out of hand once Cuffy died." Or earlier, I thought; when Mark—out of friendship and heaven knew what else—got mixed up in transporting bootleg liquor. "Suppose Amalie gets sick? Maybe she belongs in a home—a good one," I added swiftly. "You know she forgets things, and gets things twisted."

"But she's harmless! She's not hurting anybody being here, not even herself." Mark came over and took me in his arms. "If it makes you feel any better, everybody on the island knows she's here."

"Except Catriona and my father."

"Sister Janie Ruth Ford and Mr. Rafiel Jones know *all* about it. You can trust them to do the right thing, can't you? I'm not in this alone." He tilted my face up to his, his eyes fixed on mine. "Promise me you'll keep quiet about this, Tracy. Just for a little longer. Then I'll tell Catriona everything."

I nodded reluctantly, frowning. Things still didn't add up, not completely. Something didn't fit in.

"Estrada," I said at last. "He's part of this somehow, isn't he? You were supplying him with liquor, you and Cuffy, and . . . and—" I caught my breath. "He knows about Amalie, doesn't he? He found out somehow, and he's holding it over your head—"

"Shut up!" Mark said sharply. "Shut up right

there. The less you know, the safer it is. For everybody."

He pulled me close. "I'm going to get out of this, Tracy. Swear to God. It's almost finished now. Just a few more days, and it will all be over. I'm not going to do any more runs for Estrada. I told him so. I'm not going to let anyone be hurt, not you, or Amalie, or Catriona or your father. Only it would be a whole lot easier if the three of you would just leave the island for a couple of days."

He held me very tight and then, quite suddenly, he started to cry. Dry, racking sobs, like that night on the gallery. I, who had been about to weep myself, held him close. And pretty soon we were kissing instead of crying. But even while I lay in Mark's arms, responding to his kisses, that "gift" Amalie said I had was whispering something. And the cold, hard detached corner of my brain was agreeing.

The trouble on Dorr Island wasn't over. It wasn't nearly over. And some of the pieces of the puzzle were still missing.

Chapter Twenty

Three nights later Zipporah died.

For three days Zipporah had had migraine headaches. She refused to let Catriona take her to the doctor. And Catriona, suspecting the misery was mostly in her heart, and not physical, let her be. I moved through the three days like an automaton, doing my work, never speaking of the secret Mark and I were keeping.

For three nights Lucette appeared in my room sometime after midnight, crying forlornly. On the third night she wouldn't settle down at all, but paced restlessly until finally I had to put her out on the gallery and close the windows.

And the fourth morning the kitchen was deserted, and the coffeepot was cold when all of us came down. Catriona went downstairs to see how Zipporah was and came back like a wraith, white-faced.

"Kenneth? She's just lying there. I think she's dead."

My father sprang up, and Mark and I followed.

Zipporah was lying on her back, her eyes staring. The little room was very neat. There was a framed picture of Jesus on the wall, and a picture of Catriona on the bureau, and a picture of an elderly black man with a tired kind face. On the little three-legged table by the bed there was a white doily, embroidered, carefully ironed, and a gaily painted plaster lamp, and Zipporah's Bible with some feathers sticking out of it like a bookmark. I noticed these things because I was trying not to look at the bed.

I was aware of Dad bending over Zipporah, looking at her carefully, feeling for the pulse in her neck. He was that other Kenneth Fairbrother now, the professional troubleshooter, cool and methodical. Presently he straightened.

"She's dead, all right. Must have died several hours ago. Rigor mortis has practically passed. Of course, it's very hot in here."

Hot or not, I shivered.

"We'd better get a doctor anyway," my father said.

"Yes. Of course." Catriona, uncharacteristically, just stood dazedly and then wrung her hands.

"I'll go." Mark shot a look at me, and I nodded. We went out silently.

We talked little during the hour's ride. When we reached Savannah, Mark tied up at the dock. "You stay here. I'll be back with a doctor as fast as I can. If Catriona's isn't free, I'll get another." He went off at a run.

I waited until I felt I was going to jump out of my skin. Then I went ashore. It was broad daylight, there were people everywhere. I couldn't be in danger if I wandered past the waterfront shops.

I moved among groups of lively tourists, and all I could think about was death. Cuffy was dead. Zipporah was dead. Superstition said catastrophes came in threes, and Dorr Island was rife with superstition.

What was I expecting anyway, another murder?

There, I'd said it. Murder. Zipporah had said that, too, and now she was dead. I felt sick to my stomach, and wished passionately that Mark would get back with the doctor.

Maybe I'd missed their coming. Maybe they were already aboard the *Silver Cat*, waiting for me. I walked faster, and then I ran, along the street, past the lamppost where I'd first seen Cuffy, down onto the dock.

Somebody was at the boat, waiting. Not Mark. Estrada.

I saw him, and my feet stopped as if suddenly weighted with cement. And then, deliberately, I forced them on. I marched squarely up to Estrada, who was watching me insolently. "Get out of here!"

Estrada's eyes raked me, down and up. I took it without flinching. Then he laughed. "This isn't your boat."

"It isn't Mark's either. It belongs to my father and my stepmother. If you so much as touch it, I'm calling the police."

"I don't think so," Estrada said with contemptuous amusement. "Your boyfriend wouldn't like it."

"*I don't care.*" I took a deep breath and said, "I know what you've been using the *Silver Cat* for." I saw him tense, and pressed my advantage. "It's over, do you understand? That deal died with Cuffy. And I know all about that, so don't try to threaten me. Stay away from Mark. Stay away from Bonne Espérance and Dorr Island, or I'll bring in the police, and I won't care what it costs me!"

"Won't you?" Estrada asked softly. Before I knew what he was doing, he grabbed my arm. Twisted it, up against my back, so I was held forcibly close to him. "Give your boyfriend a message for me. He can't afford for the deal to end. He's in too deep. If he tries to back out, it would be just too bad for people close to him. You got that?"

For an instant we were staring at each other, eye to eye. All at once I was free. He was gone. I didn't know why until, nursing my aching arm, I looked toward the street and saw Mark and a middle-aged man coming toward us.

"Dr. Wylie, Tracy Fairbrother," Mark introduced us. "Dr. Wylie's the Dulaine family doctor. What's the matter with your arm?"

"I bumped into something," I answered evasively.

We tore out of Savannah harbor with Estrada nowhere in sight.

I'd never appreciated before how cut off island living was. Oh, we had telephones. We had boats. But a doctor was an hour's jouncing ride away, and there was no hospital or funeral home on the island.

There was a grapevine though. As we tied up at the dock we saw figures moving toward Bonne Espérance—by the great drive, through the swamp paths, and by boat. They carried flowers, the women wore hats, and they were singing. Zipporah's death was known. Perhaps my father had rung the trouble bell.

Bonne Espérance was more than ever like a house imprisoned by a spell. Dad was acting as doorman, directing traffic and taking charge of all the flowers. Sister Janie Ruth Ford, Mr. Rafiel Jones, and some of the other elders from Sister Janie's church were keeping watch with Catriona by Zipporah's bed, which was now lined with flowers. Dr. Wylie threw out everyone but Sister Janie and Catriona.

I wandered upstairs. A group of elderly islanders were holding a prayer shout in the drawing room. That was two floors up from where Zipporah lay, but I understood why Dad had shown them up there. It was the most formal, ceremonious room in the house, and so appropriate. Tears filled my eyes.

Mark came up behind me and rubbed my back. "Come on. Let's make coffee." We made gallons of coffee, and put the cakes and fruitbreads and other contributions brought by mourners onto silver plates. "Front hall's the best place," Mark decided. "Everybody goes through there on the way in or out."

He carried the coffee urns out there as I preceded him to sweep the bronze lady with her candelabra, and the Chinese embroidered mat, off the specimen table. High above us, light flooded through the ceiling dome. The chandelier had not yet been rehung.

While we were setting out cups and saucers, Catriona joined us. "Her heart stopped," she said, answering our unspoken question. "Dr. Wylie says it's not surprising. She was a lot older than I realized. Zipporah's just—always been here." Catriona's sad eyes traveled around the hall, the silver urns, the fragile china. "I remember parties here when I was little. Bini and I used to watch from the topmost landing. Dear Lord, Bini. I'll have to phone her."

"It can wait awhile. Sit down and have some coffee." I signaled Mark to pass the fruitbread. It was past noon now, and none of us had yet had breakfast.

The coffee was bitter, as Mark's always was. Catriona sipped it slowly. "If I'd only looked after Zipporah better. Maybe if I hadn't been so intent on digging out the island's secrets . . ." She made an inconclusive gesture.

"What do you mean?" Mark said sternly. He focused his dark eyes on her, forcing her to meet them. "Catriona, you said the doctor said there was nothing unusual about her dying."

"Oh, I know. But she hadn't been well. If I'd made her see a doctor more, forced her to take those blasted prescriptions instead of her home-grown cures . . ."

"Catriona, stop it."

I put my arms around her, and Mark added gruffly, "It's not always possible to hold back death. You know that."

"Now you sound like islanders." Catriona smiled weakly.

"That's no bad thing. Death be another stage of life, and Zipporah be with you alway," Sister Janie said gently, joining us. "Now, you come, child. You and your man and I got to plan the ceremonies. The family be leaving them up to us."

She led Catriona off. Mark officiated at the coffee urn as the first group of mourners came by. We worked together there for several hours, murmuring responses to what was said. From the drawing room the poignant sound of chanting spiraled down.

After a while Dad came. "You two cut out. I'll take over," he said.

Mark and I gathered used china to take with us. The late-afternoon light now touched the specimen table with splendor. I traced the odd-shaped lapis lazuli inlay with one finger. Royal-blue and scarlet, turquoise and malachite-green and crimson, all the colors of Amalie's garden. This table had stood here for two hundred years, the woods and minerals could be ten times as old, while flowers, like people, were all too mortal. "We should go tell Amalie," I said faintly.

Mark shook his head. "Gran'Amalie will already know." I knew that he was right.

We delivered the used china to the kitchen, where a group of islanders were washing dishes. Mark raided the refrigerator, and we took our plunder out to the dig. We ate cheese and bread and cold jambalaya in the foundations of an old slave cabin, and birds sang to us, and peacocks joined us to dine on crumbs. We scarcely spoke; we scarcely touched. We didn't need to.

When we went back to Bonne Espérance, we found it a house of shadows. Dad and Mr. Rafiel Jones had delivered Zipporah's body to the mainland on the *Silver Cat*. She would come back from the mortuary tomorrow morning, to lie in state in the drawing room for a day of mourning, and at sunset would be buried in the Gullah cemetery. "It won't be the first time there's been a laying-out in the drawing room," Catriona said sadly.

Night fell. We ate in the kitchen, an odd mixed-up dinner of food brought by mourners, just as if Catriona were Zipporah's daughter. Zipporah's daughter-in-law's cottage was also a designated mourning house, where the real relatives gathered, but it was too small to hold more than a dozen people at a time, Mark said. Soon after our meal was finished, he disappeared.

"Let him go. He's probably out with the island men," Catriona said heavily. "I remember, on the night before funerals, they used to keep their own watch around Zipporah's husband's still. But that was in the old days."

"Then at least we don't have to worry about revenuers," Dad said, making a joke. I looked away.

Dawn came. I found Lucette snuggled in bed with me; she'd come like a ghost and hadn't even waked me. She left by way of the gallery as soon as I got up.

The day passed in a daze. There were the sounds of soft footsteps, and endless hands to shake, and rhythmic keening, and the scents of flowers—Zipporah's coffin, brought by Shadow and the wagon from the dock, was covered with flowers. It lay open on trestles in the drawing room, and she received more flowers. Just before it was to be driven in state to the church, a tall, slim black woman in a stunning black linen suit came up the steps. Zipporah's lawyer granddaughter from Chicago. She went straight into Catriona's arms.

"Bini. Oh, Bini," Catriona whispered.

"The plane was delayed. Isaac met up with me in Atlanta; he's gone straight on to the church." Isaac Bayne was Bini's brother, the famous jazz musician. He played his blues horn at the funeral.

Isaac had to leave for a concert gig soon after the burying, but Bini was spending the night at Bonne Espérance. She and Dr. Wylie sat down with us in the library after everyone else had left.

"I'd better do something about dinner. There must be food left," Catriona said without moving. I was about to say Mark and I would see to it, when Bini interrupted.

"Never mind food. I want to know what happened. First Cuffy dies, now Grandmammy. And all I kept hearing this afternoon was how the spirits aren't at peace." She turned to Dr. Wylie, her face rigid. "You signed the death certificates, Doctor! Heart failure? In both an eighty-year-old woman with no previous history of heart attacks and a twenty-two-year-old young man with the build of a boxer? Why weren't there autopsies?"

Chapter Twenty-one

There was a shocked silence. Then Mark and the doctor both spoke at once.

"Stop acting like a lawyer—"

"Shut up, boy," Dr. Wylie interrupted firmly. He turned to Bini. "There wasn't any call for autopsies, Miss Bayne. Not unless you're looking to set off a scandal that would've broken your grandmother's heart."

"*What?*" It was Catriona who said that, not Bini.

"By all the laws of physiology and psychology, both deaths were natural, all things considered." The doctor reached in his pocket and pulled out official papers, which he passed to Bini. "Here are the death certificates. Translated, they say death by drowning followed by heavy drinking, and heart failure. Did you really want them to say suicide?"

"What the hell does that mean?" Mark shouted.

"It means that Cuffy as good as killed himself with all the stuff he was taking in. Even a boxer's body won't sustain that kind of abuse." Dr. Wylie transferred his gaze to Bini and Catriona. "Look, the kid stank of

140

bootleg liquor. I don't know where he got it; I don't want to know. Everybody in Savannah knows he's been wandering around for months now like a zombie. Which would you rather have as the official verdict: that he drowned accidentally after imbibing, or that he was poisoned by a batch of bad hooch? I tipped the police to keep an eye out for a still, so I've done my duty. And the islanders—hell, they'll have caught on right away; they'll police their own people so no one else gets hurt."

"And Zipporah?" Catriona asked tightly.

Dr. Wylie hesitated. "I know you're going to take this hard," he said at last. "I kept quiet because Zipporah insisted. But she wouldn't want you to go around blaming yourself for not taking better care of her. Zipporah had cancer. Inoperable. She's known it for a couple of years."

That explained the headaches, I thought in the shocked silence. "That's why you let her have her own way about medication, and those darn teas," Catriona whispered. The doctor nodded.

"Couldn't do any harm, and if they made her feel better . . . That's why I let her go back to working here too. She wanted to die with her boots on, and when she couldn't work, she wanted to join her ancestors. You know Gullah Christianity. Past, present, and future, life and death, are all one. Maybe her blood pressure finally did her in; maybe she worked too hard. Maybe it was the cancer, sooner than I thought, or her mind told her it was time to die and she believed it into happening. Or maybe she helped it along someway with her backlog of pills. You know her church considers suicide a sin. I wasn't about to violate that old lady's dignity by prying further than I had to, when it wasn't necessary." He looked at

Bini. "Now, Miss Lawyer, you still want to make a federal case out of it?"

Bini shook her head. But there was a look in her eyes that said she didn't buy the explanation, not completely. Of the doctor's actions, yes, but not of Zipporah's death. Neither did I. A part of my mind kept remembering Zipporah's enormous inner power, the way she'd said *murder* and predicted further deaths, the way she'd given Mark that ultimatum.

In the morning Bini left, after making Catriona promise to call her if there were anything at all that she could do. Catriona nodded silently. She was still in shock. While Mark was taking Bini to the mainland in the *Silver Cat*, Catriona went into her study and stood looking around it blankly.

"What do you want to do?" I asked. "Research, or transcribe notes, or work at the dig?" Work would be the best therapy for us both.

Catriona shook her head. "I don't want to see the dig. Not for a while. It's too much like a graveyard. If I'd spent less time on this project of mine, and more with Zipporah . . ."

"You mustn't allow yourself to think like that," Dad said. "It's not scientific. It's not healthy. That's exactly why autosuggestion is thought responsible for deaths in primitive, or perhaps I should say mystical, cultures. Go back to work, that's the way to restore normalcy again." Following his own advice, he went into the library and became very busy with his book notes.

Dad might be stirring things up with his book, as Mark had claimed, but I was sure by now that it was by his presence on the island. Not by the book's contents. Was that also true about Catriona's work? Or did she, like Zipporah, know dangerous secrets? I looked at the slim blond woman, such a curious mixture of spirituality and science, with whom I'd come to feel such a rapport, and I couldn't tell.

We worked in the study all day after all, Catriona and I, but we didn't accomplish much.

The house was very silent. That startled me when I realized it in late afternoon. For the past few days it had been so filled with people. Now it was deserted, except for Catriona and Dad and me, and the dying flowers. Mark was still out, Zipporah was gone forever, though her presence lingered, and no mourners came.

Mark just looked at me when I mentioned it that evening. He'd come back in time for dinner, as usual with no explanation of his absence, but bringing some fresh fish, which we cooked. It was a welcome change from the spicy funeral meats.

"Haven't you figured it out?" he asked, referring to our new isolation. "Bonne Espérance has got bad karma. Or whatever the right Gullah term for that is; I forget. Dulaines came back to Dorr Island and waked the sleeping cat. Gran'Amalie's got herself a silver cat and it goes prowling, just like the cat in the legend. Oh, sure, Lucette's a real cat, not a spirit. It's probably always been a real cat people have seen. But Lucette's here, and my cousin Cat Dulaine is here. And two people have died."

"The bad karma on the island comes from your friends Cuffy and Estrada, and their business enterprise!" I flared. "*That's* what's bad bad!"

"I told you, Estrada's not my friend!" Mark's eyes narrowed abruptly. "I forgot! What was he doing talking to you by the boat the day Zipporah died."

"He was sending you a message. The deal's not

over. He said you're in too deep. I told him it *was* over, that I knew everything, and if he didn't get lost, I'd go to the police—*OH!*"

I broke off with a gasp because Mark had grabbed me, unknowingly right in the same place Estrada had. Mark's face had altered terribly. "Tracy, think hard! Exactly what did you say to him? It's important!"

I parroted it dumbly, as accurately as I could remember.

"What did he say? Tracy, think!"

"He—he said—" I faltered. "He said you were in too deep. That you can't afford to back out—it would be just too bad for people close to you. . . ."

Mark let go of my arm. I rubbed it, wincing, and he made a sound and took me in his arms. "I'm so sorry. I never should have let you get into this."

"You didn't. I was just there. Or . . . I got myself in, for the same reasons you did with Cuffy."

We clung together for several minutes, feeling cold. Then Mark put me from him, gently. "You have to promise me something. You're not to go out of this house without me. Me, or your father. Not anywhere, do you understand? I'm going to settle this." His face twisted. "I've just got a—a couple of problems I've got to solve before I can. And I can't handle any of it if I'm worrying about your safety."

"Mark, you don't think . . . !"

"Don't you realize yet that the more you know, the more you're in danger? You've got to promise me!" Dazedly I promised.

It was a promise I did not mean to keep.

Chapter Twenty-two

I couldn't just stay in the house and hide. I was involved deeply, for a lot of reasons. One was because *Mark* was involved—I couldn't walk away from him any more than he could have walked away from Cuffy. Another was that our coming here, Dad and Catriona and I, had constituted a threat to Estrada. And third was *my* threat to Estrada.

I'd said I'd go to the police. I'd said I knew about the deal—what was going on. I'd meant Cuffy's illegal moonshine business. But suppose that wasn't *all* that was going on—and the fear in Mark's voice had convinced me that it wasn't. Suppose Estrada thought I knew the rest, and would kill to keep me quiet?

I couldn't wait like a sitting duck for him to try to kill me. Or Mark.

Suppose he'd killed already. Cuffy. Zipporah. Estrada wouldn't kill just to protect a moonshine operation, would he?

The doctor hadn't breathed one hint of foul play in either of those deaths. But I remembered, sickly,

145

the coiled tension that had been in Mark when the deaths were questioned.

The next day, after a sleepless night, I did what I should have done a long time back. I went to consult my father.

Mark was out on one of those unexplained boat trips—I suspected, to see Estrada. That was partly what motivated me; I had all too vivid images of Mark's body turning up somewhere in a Savannah alley. Catriona was immersed in paperwork in her study, so she was safe enough; once she settled down like that, she was lost to the world for hours. I took my father up to the ballroom, where the only door gave onto the stairwell, no one could walk in on us through the galleries, and we could see from the windows whether the *Silver Cat* returned.

And I told him. Everything.

My father's face became graver and graver as the story progressed.

"I can tell you one thing," he said at last. "There's nothing in my book that could bring goon squads, or any other killer, looking for me. Anyway, *I* haven't been a target. So whatever's set the wheels in motion has to be on the island. Either Cuffy's deal, or the fact that we're here and likely to find it out."

"Estrada thinks I've already found it out."

"So you said." Dad looked at me. "You want me to go to the police with you? Or for you? We have to report Estrada's threat and the bootlegging, Tracy."

"Not yet. Please, not yet. Mark's trying to get out of it, and—" I took a deep breath and grasped at straws—"we don't have any proof yet anyway. About the still, or—or the deaths. The police wouldn't take us seriously without evidence. We'd just be starting rumors."

"They'd take Estrada seriously, I'd like to bet. From what I know of the type, he probably is well-known to them." Dad looked at me, and his face softened. "Okay, honey. I know. You want to nail down extenuating circumstances for Mark. I hope we can, myself. What do you want me to do, look for evidence?"

"I was . . . hoping we could look for proof those *were* natural deaths."

"You have to keep an open mind in an investigation, honey," Dad said gently.

But he did help me. I told him about the conversation I'd overheard between Mark and Zipporah, and how she'd been convinced Cuffy's death was murder. How she knew what was going on and was threatening to tell if Mark did not.

"Zipporah was no fool," Dad said. "She would have known suspicions and superstition would have been laughed at by the police. Maybe she had proof somewhere."

We went downstairs and we searched Zipporah's room. Or rather, Dad searched, and I followed his instructions. Fortunately most of Zipporah's possessions had not yet been removed—only the china and photographs that had been distributed on her grave.

"I saw those photographs," Dad commented. "They were just portraits of members of her family. Nothing incriminating in them." He picked up Zipporah's Bible, and it fell open to the Twenty-third Psalm. Dad looked at the feathered bookmark, frowning.

"I know what this is. It's a talisman against evil. Zipporah must have believed she was in danger."

We went through Zipporah's drawers. At first we found nothing surprising except for a lacy black silk slip wrapped carefully in tissue. I blinked, and Dad shook his head ruefully. "Catriona sent her that from Paris, when we were on our honeymoon. It looks as though she never got to wear it."

In a metal box were Zipporah's home remedies, jars of salve and a bottle marked FOR COUGHS and small packets of herbs, probably medicinal teas and poultices. There were more little bundles of feathers, some tied with silk cords, in the bottom drawer. And with them, a curious little glass vase, double-spouted. Exactly like the one I'd found in Mark's bedroom. Dad turned it around in his fingers. "This may be some kind of a talisman too. We'd better ask Catriona."

We took the vase and the feathers and the metal box with us when we left the room, locking the door behind us. "I'll take these to town and lock them in my safe-deposit box as soon as Mark brings the *Silver Cat* back," Dad said.

Other than those things, we'd found nothing. "We'll try the other places she may have hidden things," Dad said, and together we searched the cellars. Dad's mouth tightened when I showed him the cut wire in the chandelier. "This *is* evidence. But it's probably safer here than anywhere else we might hide it."

The only thing unexpected in the cellars was some evidence of rat infestation. Dad said he'd get the exterminators, but not till after the current situation was cleared up; they might stumble into something. I was just as glad they wouldn't be around with their poisons while we might need to get to the evidence of the chandelier wire.

We went back upstairs and, after Dad had put our booty temporarily in a locked desk drawer, searched the kitchen and the pantry. Then we went up to the top floor and searched the ballroom, the governess's room, and the nursery. Nothing suspicious. The other rooms were locked.

"Catriona has the keys to the storerooms," Dad said. "I don't know whether she has a duplicate of the one to Mark's room."

I swallowed. "I know how to get in there with a hatpin."

Dad glanced at me. "Good girl. It's better to know than be afraid of knowing, isn't it?" This time he worked the hatpin.

Mark's room looked exactly as it had before, except that there were no magazines on the bed, and no little vase beneath it—or anywhere. Dad did the searching, swiftly and skillfully, while I tried not to watch.

We went out, locking up behind us. "I'll ask Catriona," Dad was just starting to say, when Catriona herself appeared on the stairs.

"Ask me what? Tracy, I'm going to have a look through the storerooms. There's a map of the islands somewhere that I remember, and I need it. Want to come along?"

A look passed between Dad and me. *Keep your eyes open*, Dad's look said, and mine said, *I will*. We wouldn't have to make Catriona's grief worse with our suspicions, after all. Dad went downstairs. I went with Catriona into the closed, slant-walled rooms smelling of dust and pomander balls and lavender.

It was like going through the strata of an archaeological dig—the strata of the Dulaine family. We found, incredibly, the velvet suit of the St. Pierre portrait. "Bini and I used to dress up in this when we weren't too scared," Catriona said, and showed me a slit in one sleeve, supposedly from a duel. There were wedding dresses of several generations of Dulaine brides.

"Too bad I didn't have this in Paris. Not that I could have gotten into it." Catriona held up a dress of rotting satin, its crinolined skirt festooned with orange blossoms that still gave off a faint perfume.

The dust was a blessing; it meant I could tell easily which piles and boxes had been touched recently. Anything about Cuffy's operation that Zipporah might have hidden here would have had to be recent. I went through the possible boxes, copying my father's professional technique as accurately and swiftly as possible. Catriona didn't seem to find anything strange about this. Probably she was used to scientific methods.

"This is most likely what we've been looking for," she said with relief when we had moved a pile of heavy draperies. A group of framed pictures stood stacked behind them. She began to go through them as I shook out the drapes, disturbing a pale yellow moth, and then refolded them.

"This is what I've been after!" Catriona's voice, for the first time in days, had a lilt to it. I went to stand beside her. She had pulled out a mahogany frame containing a delicately drawn pen-and-ink map. *Isle d'Or, known as Dorr Island. Sea Islands, Georgia. 1819.*

The parchment was yellow with age, but the watercolors were only faintly faded. "See the birds in the margins? There's a family rumor that Audubon drew the map while he was a houseguest at Bonne Espérance. And there, worked into the curlicues of the border, is the Silver Cat."

I admired the map, noting mentally that it would come in handy if a search for Cuffy's still proved necessary. "I'm taking this down. I want to compare the indications of buildings on it with those on the 1858 map I've been using. You want to come now, or poke around and lock up later?" Catriona asked.

"Later," I murmured, continuing through the stack of pictures.

And then I stopped. "Catriona, who is this?" I asked in a voice I barely recognized as my own.

Catriona came to stand beside me. "Oh!" she exclaimed with pleasure. "I'd forgotten that was up here. That's my Grandmother Dulaine, done in pastels when she was about fourteen. Poor Grandmamma, she died in a nursing home while I was living overseas. She was beautiful, wasn't she?"

I could only nod. The girl in the picture was indeed beautiful. She was also, except for the lack of wrinkles, the spitting image of Amalie.

Chapter Twenty-three

Somehow I made the appropriate remarks. Somehow I took the keys from Catriona, and promised faithfully I'd lock up after myself. Then Catriona went downstairs, and I locked myself in the attic and continued with my search. And my mind was whirling.

Amalie was Catriona's grandmother. She had to be. That made her Mark's great-grandmother, didn't it? He called her *Gran*'Amalie. So did Sophra, but that could just be a courtesy title.

Mark had liberated Amalie from a nursing home. Catriona said her grandmother had died in a nursing home.

I could picture several different threads, all twisting together. Cuffy's "business," and his dying. Estrada's threats. Mark. Zipporah's knowledge, her ultimatum, and her dying. Amalie. The common link had to be right under my nose somewhere, but I couldn't see it.

I went downstairs eventually without having pieced together anything more. It was now lunchtime, and

Dad was getting angry because Mark, or more accurately the *Silver Cat*, had not returned. He wanted to get the objects we'd found safely off the island. Every ten minutes he tried the number of the *Silver Cat*'s cellular phone, but there was no answer.

"You're as restless as a June bug," Catriona said finally. "Why?"

"I want to get to the bank before it closes." Dad showed her the objects, without explaining exactly how they'd come into our hands, and Catriona's eyes darkened.

"Definitely those feathers are a charm. I'm not sure what that glass thing is. Probably a bud vase someone sent her." Zipporah had frequently received gifts from Bini and her brother in their travels. "It looks vaguely familiar, but I don't know why. It's not a talisman." She looked sad over the herbs. "Poor Zippy, trying to hold back death with thyme and balm—yes, lock them away, just in case there's ever any question."

I could see in her eyes that there was no question for Catriona. She concurred with Dr. Wylie's conclusions. Zipporah had been a proud woman, independent. She wouldn't have wanted a lingering death.

Amalie would know about that, I thought.

Amalie—

All at once my heart started pounding.

I ate lunch with Dad and Catriona, saying little. Dad finally reached Mark aboard the *Silver Cat* and told him in no uncertain terms to come home. Afterward Catriona and I hunted up cartons in the cellar, and we packed Zipporah's things for her daughter-in-law to pick up later.

"We might as well get it over with," Catriona said heavily. "It won't be any easier later. I have to do *something*." I understood what she meant. Work

with your hands was supposed to keep you from thinking too much. In this case it didn't succeed too well.
I was uncomfortable, packing side by side with Catriona and trying to keep off the subject of Amalie,
and a few other things besides. As for Catriona—

Catriona, in the middle of packing Zipporah's
little collection of photographs, suddenly turned to
me. "Tracy? Do *you* think there's any connection?"

"Connection?" I parried.

"It keeps going through my mind. I'm trained to
look for patterns, and it just seems too much of a
coincidence. Cuffy, then Zipporah. And the chandelier." Catriona's eyes were haunted. "And the way
Mark's been behaving. So secretive; those wild flashes
of mood. I didn't want to say anything to your father,
not yet. I don't even want to think it, but—Tracy,
you're closer to him than I am. Do you think there's
anything—"

"I'm not sure," I said to cut her off.

"Neither am I," Catriona said, looking pale. "But
I can't help thinking."

Neither, unhappily, could I.

We finished stripping Zipporah's room. Catriona,
still restless, decided to drive the boxes over to their
destination. She left in the wagon. Mark returned, as
usual without explanation, and Dad was waiting for
him on the dock, with the objects we'd found packed
innocuously in a legal file case. Dad at once took off
for Savannah—it was too late now to get into the bank,
but he thought he could put the file case in a friend's
safe.

So I was alone in the house when Mark returned.
He climbed the front steps and stood looking at me,
sitting on a rocker on the gallery. He looked tired to

death, and his eyes were anxious. It occurred to me that in the weeks I'd known him, never once had I seen him when he wasn't like a caged and deeply troubled panther about to spring. I wondered what he was like when he was completely carefree.

Then I looked at the black hair, wet with sweat and spray, and it was all I could do not to brush it back from the sunburned forehead and those eyes. If I felt like this now, after all his moods and anger, nothing could shake me. We were bound together by everything that had passed between us.

The expression in his eyes said, more clearly than words, that he knew it too. Then his gaze slid to the purple bruise on my arm, and he drew his breath in sharply. "I'm sorry. I never meant to hurt you."

"You didn't. At least not just you. Estrada did that when I challenged him in Savannah." I saw Mark's face alter, and said hastily, "Where were you?"

"Where do you think? Having it out with him. Don't ask!" He forestalled the question in my eyes. "I promised you everything would be all right soon, and it will be. Just as soon as I get a few loose ends tied up and some arrangements made. In the mean-time . . ."

He walked away from me to the railing, and stood staring off toward the dock.

"In the meantime what?" I asked ominously. "You're not going to say 'Business as usual.' *Mark!* You don't mean to go on running moonshine to the mainland for Estrada! Anyway"—I was grasping at straws—"anyway, with Cuffy gone there's nobody to make more, you said the recipe was secret."

Mark walked away.

"You're not trying to tell me *you*—"

"I'm trying very hard not to tell you anything," Mark said tautly. "That's the only way to keep you safe."

Only I wasn't safe, not after what I'd said to Estrada, and we both knew it.

Mark went downstairs, and I went up to my room to lie down with what was suddenly a raging headache.

Ten minutes later Mark burst in on me. "What's happened to all Zipporah's things?"

"Catriona's taken them over to Cuffy's mother."

"All of them?"

I sat up and I said, very distinctly, "No, not all. Not Zipporah's talismans against evil, not her prescription medications, not the . . . the herb medicines your great-grandmother made up for her."

"*What did you say?*"

"You heard me."

Mark stared at me. Then, all at once, his tension escaped like air from a pricked balloon. "I'm glad you know," he said simply. "I wanted to tell you. I didn't dare take the chance. How did you find out?"

I told him about the picture.

Mark's head jerked up. "Catriona?"

"She doesn't know. But, Mark, you have to tell her!"

"I know, I know. I was just going to, when all this started happening."

"I still don't see why you didn't from the start."

"I didn't even know Catriona in the old days. I was a little kid. She inherited the place, but she let everything go to pot while she lived abroad. I thought it was *safe* to bring Gran'Amalie here! When Catriona showed up, with a husband, it knocked me for a loop."

"You should have told her right then. You should

have told her in the first place. She'd have helped you get Amalie out of that nursing home legally."

"I couldn't know that, could I?" Mark stroked the pale blue satin comforter with a grimy finger. "By the time they got here, I was in too deep."

"Cuffy and Estrada."

Mark nodded. "Estrada found out who Amalie was and how she'd gotten to the island. When I tried to back out on him, he threatened to call social services and get her put away. That old boat of mine—I thought at the time Estrada might have blown that up as a warning. I'm sure of it now."

"All the more reason you've got to tell Catriona right away. About everything."

"I can't! Not till I've got all the bases covered."

The little French clock on the mantel chimed, and Mark sprang up. "Lord, I've wasted time, I've forgotten— Tracy, those talismans and things. Where are they?"

"Safe. Dad's taken them to Savannah."

"*What?*"

"Mark, calm down and listen! What the doctor said about how Cuffy and Zipporah died—it was a good idea to let that be, especially the death certificates, to avoid suspicion. But Bini didn't buy it; you could tell she didn't. Neither did I. Neither do Dad or Catriona, not anymore, and you don't either. If Zipporah was murdered, the logical way was through the medications. So Dad took all the stuff away. Not to the police, not yet. But where they can get them."

Mark, galvanized, grabbed the phone. "Call him! Track him down somewhere and—tell him whatever story you want, but get them back here. Especially the medications. We've got to get rid of them!"

"We've got to turn them over to the police! Don't you understand? It's no good—going it alone like you've been doing. So you're mixed up in transporting bootleg liquor. You didn't know what you were doing when it started, and it's not as if it were drugs—" I broke off, startled, as the memory of Mark's extremes of mood flooded over me. "Mark, you don't do drugs?"

"No way!" Mark said violently. "I've seen too much. Tracy, listen—"

"No. *You* listen. You tell Catriona about Amalie, and then Estrada doesn't have anything to hold over your head. Transporting moonshine's nothing compared to his being a suspect in a murder. Two murders," I corrected, remembering Cuffy. "We probably can't do a thing about proving the first one now, but the second's different. If Zipporah's pills were tampered with, Estrada had to have been behind it. He's the evil she was threatening to expose. If we get them analyzed—"

"You still don't get it, do you?" Mark shouted in despair. "Pills would have been too obvious. Estrada wouldn't have risked it. Besides, there was no way to be sure she'd take them. If Zipporah was poisoned it had to have been by the herbs. Not deliberately! I think Gran'Amalie poisoned her by mistake!"

Chapter Twenty-four

"That's what Estrada told you today, wasn't it?" I whispered. "You accused him of having something to do with Zipporah's death, and he said it was Amalie. That's it, isn't it?"

"Grandfather had Amalie committed to an institution because she was a danger to herself," Mark said quietly. "Do you want to take a chance the authorities won't think she's become a danger to others too? You got sick from her tansy cakes and tea, remember? Zipporah was old, and dying, and Gran'Amalie doled out old wives' remedies. And her eyes are bad, and maybe she got poisonous herbs mixed up with harmless ones. There's a lot of foxglove in her garden, and foxglove's really belladonna. Digitalis. Zipporah had a bad heart, among other things."

"Dear God," I said softly.

"You'd better believe it. Estrada said nobody'd think for a minute that anyone but Amalie was responsible," Mark said miserably. "And he's right. They wouldn't. Not if there were no—outside poison put into anything. How long do you think Gran'Amalie would survive in an institution for the criminally insane?"

"It couldn't come to that!"

But Mark was in no mood to listen to reason. It was very evident his mind was made up that Amalie had been responsible—not deliberately, but responsible all the same. I didn't believe it, even after the tansy and the tea. But then, Amalie wasn't my greatgrandmother. I hadn't taken responsibility for her; could I take responsibility for turning her in?

"Exactly what are you planning to do about all this?" I asked.

Mark looked at me gratefully. "Sister Janie's been making arrangements for Gran'Amalie to stay in a private rest home not far from Savannah. If we can talk her into going there, just for a while—then I'll tell Catriona about how I moved her, and if Gran'Amalie starts murmuring anything about things she's done here, everyone will be sure she's imagining things. None of the islanders will give away the fact she's been here. They all love her. Estrada won't be able to prove a thing, and in the meantime I'll have a chance to get out from under him."

"You could start," I said pointedly, "by torching Cuffy's still. That would cut off Estrada's supply. I still don't see why you're so important to Estrada that he'd risk all this anyway."

"Private island. Off the coast. Will you *please* get on that phone and find your father?"

"No. But I'll give you the rest of the week to get Amalie away from here. *If* you swear by your life you'll stay away from Estrada in the meantime." The medications, doctored or innocent, would be safe enough in Dad's friend's safe for a few more days.

Mark tensed, and I waited anxiously for his reply. I knew how I must sound to him—the do-gooder who had to mess up his plans. But I didn't care. If our love, or whatever it was between us, couldn't take this, then it wasn't worth having.

Our eyes locked for a moment, and he nodded. Then he turned abruptly on his heel and strode away.

I didn't phone Dad, but I didn't tell him about our conversation either. I felt as if I'd fallen into a swamp again, a swamp in which there was no right or wrong but only a choice between evils.

Dinner that night was somber. It felt awful being in that golden room without Zipporah coming in and out, but we made ourselves do it. Otherwise, as Catriona said, it would get harder and harder. The conversation, such as it was, concerned Dad's book. He'd seen his lawyer during the afternoon, and the lawyer wanted him to come back in the morning to discuss a contract for some newspaper articles.

"I think I'll go with you," Catriona said. She looked at me. "Want to come? We can go shopping. A day off the island might do you good."

I shook my head. No way did I want to risk running into Estrada when Catriona was around. Besides, I had hard thinking to do, and I wanted to be alone to do it. Even now that I knew the truth about Amalie, there was still a piece missing somewhere. Why was Estrada risking so much for the sake of maintaining his island source? The profit in it couldn't be that great, could it? I wondered again if drugs were involved. But Mark was so against drugs, how could that be?

My headache was back in full force, but I didn't get to sleep till late. I woke again, a few hours later, to a familiar rumbling on my chest. Lucette was back, and purring.

I scratched her ear, feeling as if I wanted to cry.

"I wish you could talk. You see darn near everything that goes on on the island, don't you? You probably know where that still is, even." If I could find it, I thought grimly, I'd put a torch to it myself.

"*Mrowr,*" Lucette complained, and batted at my ear. Her blue eyes glowed at me through the darkness. I reached over and snapped on the light, now wide-awake.

Lucette had no intention of letting me get up. She settled on my chest again, butting at my chin. Then rolled over, looking at me coyly from beneath one arm. "*Rrrrrr?*" she trilled.

"You sure are acting spaced-out tonight," I laughed, and Lucette trilled again and rolled back over. There was something in her mouth, and her conversation came around it oddly.

"Okay, what have you got that you shouldn't have?" I asked.

For answer she dropped the object on my bare skin. A small, roughly shaped lump of a whitish substance, about the size of a large candy. Rock candy. Or—

All of a sudden my heart and pulses both were pounding. I reached out gingerly, and picked the lump up, and looked at it. And then, despite the fact that it had been in Lucette's mouth, I tasted it.

I wasn't at all sure what the taste I expected would be like, but it wasn't candy. Neither was this. It made my tongue feel numb.

Crack. Cocaine, in a form that was one of the most lethal drugs ever known. And the most addictive. And the most profitable.

Thanks to the whisper of Amalie's little cat, I had the final piece of the puzzle at last, the piece that locked all the other ones together. Not bootleg liquor running at all, but drugs. Hard drugs, brought in as cocaine probably from beyond the ten-mile limit. Brought in on the *Silver Cat*—I'd been told how far and fast she could travel. Cuffy'd had a factory on the island, all right, but not a moonshine factory.

Cuffy—I sat up so abruptly that I knocked Lucette and the lump of crack overboard. Lucette complained, and scrambled up, and I rescued the lump of crack quickly. Sat there holding it, locked in both my hands, in the old room in the old house that had already known so much violence and so much evil.

Cuffy had died without a mark on him, and with a look of horror on his face. I remembered hearing about a young basketball player with an athlete's body who'd died like that. Snap, bang! A rush of adrenaline that the heart couldn't handle. And instant death.

Cuffy hadn't just been a dealer; he'd been an addict. And Mark—I knew without being told—had been protecting him. Protecting, trying to wean him away—from the addiction, and from the dealing. And all the while in over his head, because he'd been lured into the boat runs before he knew what product he'd been transporting. When he thought it was just moonshine.

Not for one minute did I believe Mark was involved with crack in any other way. I'd seen his face when he'd said he didn't do drugs, that he knew too much. *I should have known then he meant somebody real close to him was an addict*, I thought.

I should have known when I found that little glass vase hidden under the bed of Mark's locked room. Not a vase. A crack pipe. No wonder it had looked vaguely familiar to me, though not to Dad or Catriona. As an ordinary middle-class girl in a nice ordinary American high school, I'd been closer to drugs than they'd been as adults overseas. I'd seen the documentaries, heard the stories about kids who used drugs at school.

"Oh, Mark," I thought sickly. No wonder he hadn't been able to disentangle himself from Estrada! No wonder Dorr Island—unoccupied except by the Gullah—was so important to Estrada. With Cuffy dead, there wasn't a way in the world Mark could prove he hadn't gone into the drug racket with his eyes wide open!

And then, like a breath of fresh air coming through the windows, I had a vision of Amalie smiling at me in her enchanted garden. I had a memory of Amalie's voice saying, "Good is always stronger than evil." And I knew what I was going to do.

I fell asleep again with the lump of crack tucked in my nightstand drawer and Lucette cuddled comfortingly at my feet.

When I woke the next time the sun was streaming in, Lucette was gone, and the house was very silent. I dressed, hid the lump of crack very carefully down at the bottom of my jar of bath salts, and went downstairs.

A note for me, in a sealed envelope, lay on the kitchen table:

Tracy—

Gone to mainland with your dad & C. on you know what business. Lock yourself in and BE CAREFUL!

XXXX
M.

I didn't lock myself in. After breakfast, and after remembering the effect the Georgia sun had on me, I borrowed one of Catriona's floppy hats. Then, feeling rather ridiculous, I got a small, sharp knife from a kitchen drawer and tucked it inside my bra. Just in case I'd need it. And then, locking the house behind me, I went out, saddled Shadow, and rode over to the other side of the island, praying every inch of the way.

I went first to Mr. Rafiel Jones, and under the pretense of asking about island history, I got him talking about Zipporah's husband's still. He told, as he always did, great stories.

"Where was it?" I asked, I hoped casually.

"Lord, child, that was the biggest joke of all. It was in that old deserted cottage, the one the first Dulaines lived in, and Mr. Dulaine, the one that was living in the big house at the time, he never caught on at all." Mr. Rafiel Jones laughed. "Wouldn't do nobody no good to try that again now! The cottage be 'most all fall down."

I knew that was true. I'd seen it. Wherever Cuffy's factory—crack, moonshine, or both—was, it wasn't there.

I went next to Sister Janie, and thanked her for all her help over the days of Zipporah's death ceremonies. Looking into the goodness of her eyes, I knew that Sister Janie, for all her wisdom, didn't know the nature of the evil being practiced on the island. That meant Cuffy'd been very smart, and that Zipporah had carried the secret to her grave. Out of love for Cuffy? Or for Mark? Definitely out of love for Amalie.

Sister Janie knew about Amalie. I felt suddenly, and gratefully, that I could leave the ethics of the Amalie situation in Sister Janie's hands.

I had a difficult time, though, getting away from Sister Janie's searching questions. "That Mark, he be all right now? He look like he seeing ghosts, the day of funeral."

"I'm afraid he was. Sister Janie, what should I do?"

"You get him to tell the truth. Whatever he be into.

Nothing so bad confession don't make it better. And free the soul." Sister Janie smiled. "You know, that be what the Silver Cat really come down to. Conscience."

"It's not that easy. He's worried about Amalie."

"I know. Gran'Amalie, she be stronger than he give her credit for, maybe. And wiser. He pretty young yet, you know, for all he be some man." Her dark eyes twinkled, then grew sober. "You make him take care of hisself, you hear?"

"Sister Janie—if somebody had to hide on this island—hide for safety, or hide a secret—where could they go?"

"Lord, child, I don't know noplace other folk wouldn't know. Folks that knew the island, that is." That included Estrada, I thought dully. No way did I believe Cuffy'd been able to set up a crack factory without expert assistance. "I used to hear tell of caves hereabout, back in the old smuggling days. But when there was a slave uprising once, Master had them all dynamited and that sealed them in, them and all the poor blacks hiding in them."

Another bloody chapter of island history.

Sister Janie had been scanning my face. Now she rose suddenly. "Zipporah give me something last week, something from big house she want me to keep. I think be wise I give it to you now." She went into her cottage and returned, carrying something wrapped in dark brown flannel. She laid it on her outdoor table and unwrapped it. A long rope of dark, worn leather, with nine tails, each tail tipped with a metal arrowhead that glittered in the sun.

"St. Pierre's cat-o'-nine-tail whip," Sister Janie said. "Zipporah Bayne thought it's what was used to make those marks on her grandson's face."

Chapter Twenty-five

I rode away with the whip, wrapped, tied to my saddle.

I knew where, inevitably, my next stop would be. Amalie's cottage.

Amalie was not in sight. Lucette came out to meet me, twisting around my ankles and whimpering plaintively. That must have been what had frightened me on the path that time—not a ghost cat, but Lucette, twisting against my legs so her fur barely brushed me! I followed her emphatic mewing to the cottage door.

Amalie was sitting in a rocker, her hands neatly folded, staring into space. When I finally got her to focus on me, she thought I was her mother. I kissed her, and left her, knowing there was no help for me here. Amalie had escaped, for now at least, into the only refuge open to her—the mists. Perhaps it was better that way.

I rode back to the big house, knowing nothing

more about the location of the crack factory than when
I'd started.

I had the whip. That was a very tangible piece
of evidence, and maybe it had fingerprints. But whose?
I knew that they might be Mark's. *I'd never make
Cuffy's death look like something worse than it was,*
he'd said. Had he made it look like an alcoholic drowning as a less terrible thing than a crack overdose?

I didn't have time for analysis now. I needed facts.
The remaining places to look for them were Catriona's
files—where I knew by now no information on caves
existed—and that map.

I took the map down, carefully, from the study
wall where Catriona had hung it. Pored over it with
a magnifying glass, until I knew every line and curve
of coast and swamp. There were no caves marked. I
checked the date of the slave uprising in the files. It
was twenty years later than the date on the map, and
no cave was mentioned—only a "cottage" that had
been "burned out." So much for the universal urge
to pretty up history. It hadn't been prettied up by
Catriona; the account was taken from a Savannah
newspaper and from an ancestor's journal, but the end
result was the same.

I put the notes back in the file, closed the file
drawer, and returned the map to its hook, feeling lower
by the minute. Maybe I should just turn the lump of
crack over to my father, and let Amalie and Mark take
their chances.

Maybe I'd better put St. Pierre's whip away someplace safer than the hall table where I'd left it.

I went back to the hall, noting absently that the
bronze lady and her Chinese mat had never been
returned to the center table since the funeral. I'd laid
the whip on the bare table, and it was a good thing

the whip was wrapped, because I'd been told how valuable that table was. Valuable not just for its component worth, but because it had been made for St. Pierre.

I locked the whip in the bottom drawer of Catriona's files, and located the bronze lady, and took her and the Chinese mat back to the hall. There were a couple of marks from coffee cups on the table top, so I went for a damp paper towel and began, carefully, to remove them. The tabletop was, in its own way, beautiful, at least its colors were, even though the design was such an odd, unbalanced shape. Not concentric, geometrically divided circles, as most specimen tables were, but almost like a map.

Almost like a map.

I stared at it, and the pattern of the map I'd been studying and the pattern of the table became one.

Turquoise-green for the sea, light and dark in turns, sometimes in the exact places where Mark had pointed out that the water became shallower or deeper. Lapis-blue where the creeks ran, and where the little pond was behind Mr. Rafiel Jones's home. Jade-green where the marsh grasses sighed, and nephrite-green for forests, malachite for swamps. Coral for the buildings of Bonne Espérance. Varicolored onyx for the slave cabins, the sites of long-ago mill and cooperage and saddlery. Carnelian for shacks (now islanders' cottages?) on the far side of the island. Amethyst for docks. Hematite—

I leaned forward, holding my breath. Hematite for caves? Yes, the silver-flecked gunmetal stone gleamed near inlets, the natural places, and twice amid the cat's-eyes that indicated dry undeveloped land, and twice ran in a thin thread to Bonne Espérance. Somebody'd told me that there used to be underground smugglers' tunnels to Bonne Espérance. One thread ran between Bonne Espérance and the main dock. I knew that dock area thoroughly. If there had been a cave there once, there was none now. The other thread—

I straightened, and as if the voice of justice were speaking to me through the mouth of the Silver Cat, I knew the exact location of Cuffy's crack factory.

I went to the dining room and got a box of matches. Then I took the cat-o'-nine-tails, went out of the house, and locked it. And then I went to Shadow, still saddled and grazing patiently.

I rode out back, past the ruins of the slave cabins. Distantly, through a gap in the forest, I could see the sea of reeds and the *Silver Cat*, rocking quietly at anchor. Dad and Catriona, and perhaps Mark, too, must have just returned. I did not want them to see me. I kept riding.

Past the place where I'd seen Cuffy's body. Past the fork in the road. Up to the ruined Dulaine cottage, with its roses and its family motto and its dark, dark memories. Slaves hiding in a cave, Sister Janie had told me. Slaves hiding in the old cottage, which was then blown up, according to the files. Both at one and the same place, according to the table made for St. Pierre, who had used the island for such dark purposes. The knife tucked in the band of my bra rasped my skin slightly as I slid down from Shadow's back. And I took the wrapped whip with me. I did not know why—instinct, or a foolish idea of self-protection.

I made my way along the worn path, across the doorstep with its sleeping cat. Dad had searched in here the night I'd found and lost a body, and seen nothing. But it had been night, and Dad had not known what to look for. I did. I went carefully, inspecting every stone, and when I reached the fireplace wall, I saw what I'd been looking for. A large block of stone in the back of the fireplace, not so firmly set as the rest.

I explored with my fingers, first the stone itself, then the surrounding ones. And, exactly as I'd seen it in some old movie, the stone block pivoted.

I was looking in, and down, at the crack factory. I'd never seen one, but I knew that was what this was. There was a table with equipment like in my school chemistry lab back home, and plastic packets filled with something white.

Plastic packets. Plastic melted when touched with heat. The pile of newspapers beneath the table would burn.

I reached down in the low neckline of my dress and groped for the box of matches. Brought it out. Took out a match, and was about to strike it.

And then arms grabbed me. A voice close to my ear said roughly, "No, you don't, babe. The fire *next* time!"

The odd phrase tugged at my memory, but I had no time to think about its source. It was Estrada's voice.

Chapter Twenty-six

"Little Miss Smart-ass. It never occurred to you there could be two exits from in there, did it?" He threw me to the ground and stood looking at me sardonically. There was a gun in his hand.

"You can't get away with this," I said stupidly.

"Oh, I think I can. I'm very good at accidents. Lady, you've become a nuisance to my business, and I can't afford it. Now, get up!"

I did so gingerly, taking my belongings with me. The wrapped whip. The matches— *Leave the matches*, the voice in my head said. *They'll prove you've been here.* I let the box of matches slide to the ground.

"Outside." Estrada jerked his head toward the doorstep. Out we went, across the threshhold with its worn carved warning. Shadow, grazing placidly, lifted his head to blink at me.

"Shadow! Go home!" I shouted.

Shadow's head jerked and he took off. Estrada laughed. "You think that nag's going to fetch help like a dog would?" I said nothing. He didn't know about my conversation with Dad about that other time.

The gun butt nudged the back of my ribs. "Move." We were around on the far side of the cottage. Still holding the gun on me, Estrada pulled a motorcycle out of the rosebushes.

"Get on! And don't try to pull a fast one. I'm very good on this baby, and I'll have the gun to your head the whole time." I got on, still clutching my bundle. The hidden knife rasped me again, but I didn't dare try to pull it. He'd have seen me.

We roared down a path through the swamp that I hadn't known about. He really was able to maneuver the cycle with one hand, keeping the gun pressed against me the whole time. I hung on for dear life.

Distantly I heard the trouble bell begin to ring.

It had no meaning for Estrada. We came out of the swamp very near the dock. Estrada killed the motor and climbed off, yanking me with him. The *Silver Cat* rocked placidly at anchor.

The fire *next* time. Now I remembered. *God send de rainbow*, the old spiritual ran, *to be a sign. No more water. De fire next time.*

"You're going to blow up the *Silver Cat*, aren't you?" I asked, quite coolly. "Just like you blew up Mark's other boat."

"Smart, aren't you? I can replace it easily. Crack's a very profitable business. What I can't afford is having people know about it. I smell one rat, I take care of it, and another pops up."

My mind wheeled crazily from rats to poison and made a sudden connection. Without thinking, I blurted it out.

"Like Zipporah? What did you do? Spray Amalie's herb patch with insecticide?"

It was a wild guess, but it struck a nerve. Estrada's face darkened. "Shut up and *move!*"

I did so. Slowly. Out of the corner of my eye I saw Mark creeping, crouching, through the marsh grass. I didn't let my eyes flicker once.

Up to the *Silver Cat*. Another power boat, probably Estrada's, rocked beside it. Estrada ignored it. "Get in." And I stepped up onto the slippery fiberglass rim of the *Silver Cat*. Stepped down. Estrada stepped in after me.

Mark sprang.

He went over the side of the boat onto Estrada's shoulders. They both went down, sprawling, into the outside seating area. Estrada's gun fell. I dove for it, and the side of Estrada's hand struck my arm like a knife blade. I screamed. Mark rolled over, reaching out.

And then, suddenly, the gun was in Estrada's hands again. He stood, legs straddled, pointing it at us both.

"Into the pilot's seat!" he snapped at Mark. "I'll kill you now if I have to, but I'd rather not."

Mark shot me an agonized look and obeyed. We both knew what Estrada was planning, even before he took one hand from the gun and reached into his pocket.

An explosion, just the way there had been with the old wooden boat. Only this time Mark and I would be in it. All Estrada's problems would be wrapped up at once. I couldn't imagine Catriona and my father staying on the island once we'd been killed. And there wouldn't be a single thing to prove any of this had happened. Who was going to look for evidence in a jar of bath salts?

Mark twisted around, and his eyes met mine. I knew what he was planning. He was going to make some kind of crazy, gallant diversion, and I was supposed to get away.

Estrada was pulling out his explosives, still watching Mark. I was only in the periphery of his vision. My right hand slid into the flannel wrappings of my bundle, and closed around something hard. The whip handle.

I shifted position, forcing Estrada to do so, too, in order to cover both of us with his aim. Estrada's back was against the side of the boat.

Mark's hand found the key of the *Silver Cat*. His foot gunned the motor.

The *Silver Cat* leaped into the air. At the same moment Estrada's gun went off. Mark cried out. In that instant before the gun swung toward me, I yanked out St. Pierre's whip and snapped it full into Estrada's face.

The nine silver arrowheads, sharp as knives, glinted like a rainbow in the afternoon sun. Estrada fell backward against the edge of the boat, his arms across his face. And I ran to him, and pushed him over into the water.

He was alive. I saw him swimming, not toward us, but toward the other boat. We had to get out of there ahead of him, and the *Silver Cat* was throbbing. I flung the whip down and bent over Mark.

He'd been shot in the shoulder and was losing a lot of blood. "Can you drive?" I shouted, and he shook his head with effort.

"Think the bullet . . . got something." His face was gray. He tried to lift himself from the seat, but couldn't, so I pushed him over into the passenger's seat. I couldn't worry whether I was hurting him.

I slid into the pilot's seat and floored the gas. This thing ran just like a car, I remembered. My hands tightened like vises around the steering wheel, and the

Silver Cat kept leaping as I headed northwest toward Savannah, using the sunset as my guide.

Behind us a motor roared. I shot a look into the rearview mirror. Estrada, as I'd known it would be. The *Silver Cat* was faster than his boat. It had to be.

Something rang. It took me a few seconds to realize it was the cellular phone. "Can you get that?" I shouted into the wind to Mark. Then I realized he had passed out.

I pried one hand from the steering wheel and grabbed the receiver. My father's voice shouted through it. *"Who is this?"*

"It's Tracy. Dad—"

"Are you all right?"

"Dad, shut up and listen! We're heading for Savannah. Mark's been shot, and there's a guy named Estrada right behind us! Call the police and the Coast Guard! Hurry!"

"Roger, over and out," said my father's government-service voice.

Estrada was gaining on us. I dared a look backward, and the look cost me precious time as the *Silver Cat* swerved off course. Estrada came up toward one side, and bullets sprayed.

I jerked at the wheel and we zoomed away again. *Don't look back. Don't worry. Remember what Amalie said about good being stronger than evil, and just keep going.*

Mark's eyes were still closed, and blood stained his blue shirt like a dark red flower unfolding. Don't think about that either.

That was how it went, zooming first right, then left, like water-skiers in a desperate race, until a helicopter hovered over us, and Coast Guard launches closed in, just as the towers of Savannah loomed.

Chapter Twenty-seven

Seven days later—or seven *nights* later, to be precise—Mark and I were sitting at the restaurant by the waterfront.

"Where it all began," Mark said. I wasn't sure whether he meant the troubles or *us*. Maybe both.

Mark's arm was in a sling to keep stress from his chest and shoulder. Otherwise he was in good shape, in better shape than in all the weeks I'd known him. His eyes were no longer haunted.

A lot had happened in those seven days. Lon Estrada was under arrest without bail. We guessed some of his "business associates" were too—the police were being pretty cagey about that. The Feds had been brought in; I knew that because two of them had been out to Bonne Espérance to question us. We gathered they were keeping the lid on everything, in hopes of catching more of the cocaine-smuggling network in their drug sweep. At any rate very little had hit the papers, to Catriona's profound relief.

The Feds and the local police, working in wary cooperation, had also swept Dorr Island. Very few people had escaped questioning, at least according to Zipporah's daughter-in-law, who had now taken over the housework at Bonne Espérance. The crack factory underneath the old Dulaine cottage had been completely dismantled. Everything in it had been impounded as evidence, and the cave had been sealed for good.

Amalie had been reunited with Catriona. Catriona had wept, and bawled Mark out, and ended by hugging him in spite of the wounds that made it difficult for him to reciprocate. She had arranged for Amalie to be admitted to a private hospital in Savannah for evaluation, and if the doctors approved, Amalie would be coming home to live with us. *Home.* Bonne Espérance felt like a home now.

Mark had had a hard week in more ways than one. He was a hero for trying to save me, but he was also involved in a very serious crime. *Crime,* singular. The authorities agreed he was not involved in Zipporah's death, nor in the actual manufacture and sale of crack. Only in the shipping end, and that under pressure of blackmail. They'd bought his insistence that he hadn't known, at the beginning, what merchandise was being shipped.

As soon as we'd known Mark was going to survive the bullet wound all right after he'd been transported to the hospital under police guard, Catriona had gone to a hospital phone and summoned Bini. Bini arrived later that night, and after interrogating Dad and Catriona and me for hours, she went into court in the morning flourishing all kinds of legal papers. She was able to have Mark kept in the hospital, though under police guard (and over Mark's indignant insistence that he was fine) until this morning. This afternoon she'd been able to get him out, on bail posted by Dad and Catriona.

He might still have to go on trial. He might get off on probation, or be charged with a much lesser crime. Mark himself, as well as character witnesses such as Sister Janie Ruth Ford and Mr. Rafiel Jones —and me—had made a favorable impression at the district attorney's office. That was another place we'd been on this hectic day. Mark's obvious revulsion at drugs, particularly crack and what it had done to Cuffy, and his eagerness to testify against Estrada now that Amalie was safe, had been impressive. The district attorney was talking about maybe dropping charges if Mark would sign up for a work-study program and do some volunteer work with kids.

Right now none of that mattered. The nightmare was over, Mark was free, and we were together. Dad and Catriona had recognized our need to be alone.

"Frankly I think they were itching to be alone too," Mark said, grinning. "Do you realize this is the first time since they got here months ago that they've had Bonne Espérance to themselves?"

"*Bonne Espérance*," I said aloud. "Good Hope. Maybe now it will be an appropriate name after all."

"If anyone can exorcise the shades of St. Pierre and his victims, it's you and Catriona," Mark said. He lifted his mug of soft drink to toast me.

"And Amalie," I said, blushing. "She's an—exorcist, too, in a way." I shivered faintly.

Mark pulled his chair around next to mine and put his good arm around me. "Don't talk about exorcists. Actually I think the spirits around Dorr Island have been kind ones. They haven't been threatening us, they've been warning and protecting."

"That's what Sister Janie says. And Amalie. 'Good is always stronger than evil.' Zipporah knew that too."

We were silent for a moment, remembering that monumental figure.

"Anyway," I said, determinedly cheerful, "*Our* Silver Cat's certainly been our good angel. I'd never have caught on about the *real* hold Estrada had on you if she hadn't shown up with that lump of crack."

"Which she probably thought was a toy, or candy," Mark finished. "Cuffy always had trouble keeping her out of that place. She could squeeze through the smallest holes in the old walls, and get in. Nosy. Cuffy was afraid Estrada would poison her."

"We've been lucky, haven't we?"

"As Zipporah would have said, *Hallelujah!*" Mark put his hand over mine. "Look, I don't care whether we have dessert, do you? Let's get out of here."

"Not quite yet," I protested. There were still questions I needed answered, and I knew that once we were back on the *Silver Cat*, cruising quietly through the moonlit waters, crime was going to be the last thing on our minds.

"Okay, shoot." Mark laughed. "No, take that word back." He rubbed his wounded shoulder gingerly. "You could do this a lot better than I can," he hinted, his dark eyes twinkling.

One question had already been definitely settled for us both. Would we still like each other, once we were back to our normal selves, the selves neither of us had had a chance to see in each other before?

As Zipporah would say, *Amen!* Also *Hallelujah!*

"I think," Mark said, demonstrating again his ability to read my mind, "I'd kind of like to go over to Sister Janie's church this Sunday."

"We'll probably be asked to give testimonies."

"I wouldn't mind."

Another silence. More remembering, but it was happy, and it was healing.

"How did you catch on about Estrada poisoning Zipporah by spraying Amalie's herb garden with insecticide?" Mark asked with respect. "I never guessed. I was pretty near you by then, hiding in the marsh, and when I heard you shout that out, I nearly freaked."

"Lucky guess. Mom used to spray her tomato plants, and I remembered the warning labels about systemic poisoning. But it was when he said 'rat' that I made the connection." I explained about Dad's discovery of rats in the cellar, privately feeling sorry that we'd have to call in the exterminators now. Those rats had helped us, after all.

"Luckily Sister Janie and Mr. Rafiel Jones knew she never did use pest sprays. And luckily you and your dad kept those herb packets." Mark shook his head. "I never guessed. I was so convinced Gran'Amalie must have been responsible."

"You were too close to see anything clearly by then. And too worried."

"You can say that again!" Mark looked at me. "I was in seeing Estrada that day. You guessed that, didn't you? I was there the other times I stood you up. Trying to force him to back off! Estrada said even if he did kill Zipporah, which he wasn't admitting, he'd be able to hang it on Gran'Amalie."

He looked off across the crowded restaurant. People were laughing and talking, being happy. A concealed spotlight glinted on the horn of the jazz soloist as he wove a haunting blues tune into the atmosphere. I knew Mark, like me, was seeing that other night. The night, as I knew now, that Cuffy had tried to warn Mark that Estrada was looking for him.

"You used the cat-o'-nine-tails on Cuffy's face, didn't you?" I asked suddenly. "You did that, and you moved Cuffy's body. To get it away from the crack factory, and Amalie's cottage."

"I had to," Mark said simply. "If anybody realized Cuffy'd died of crack, the whole thing would have blown up. I don't mean on me. I mean Gran'Amalie. Estrada was already threatening she'd be the one to pay. He'd run into her one day, and he'd made investigations. She was my weak spot, and he knew it. I think he'd have killed her, if he had to, in order to keep the crack factory in operation. Dorr Island was too valuable to him as a base of operations."

"But then Dad and Catriona came," I said. "Hence the chandelier."

"He was trying to scare them off. And scare me. It proved to me that he'd found the old tunnel, and was able to get into Bonne Espérance undetected. That meant nobody in it was safe. And by then," Mark added, smiling crookedly, "I had another weak spot. You."

I knew the rest. How Estrada had kept forcing Mark into "just one more" drug run until he'd finally made clear there wasn't going to be an ending.

And Cuffy died.

"Not murder," Mark said. "Though it might as well have been. Cuffy took the crack of his own free will." He was silent for a moment, then the shadow of his old violence burst out. "When I found out Cuffy was using it, I could have killed somebody! Estrada, anyone! Maybe I should have killed Estrada right then. It would have saved everyone a lot of grief. And saved Zipporah."

"Don't talk like that," I said swiftly. "Can't you hear what Zipporah would say? She'd rather have died herself than have you be a murderer, or be killed." As I would have, I added silently, that day Estrada shot you.

Mark looked into my eyes. "I didn't know," he said slowly, "that Cuffy was involved in drugs. In the beginning, like I said in the D.A.'s office, I thought he was peddling moonshine. Oh, sure, I knew that was illegal, but who was it hurting? Southerners have been doing that for two hundred years! I owed Cuffy a few, and I needed money, and—oh, I'll admit it. I liked the kick I got from it. Then I found out."

"How?"

"Would you believe Lucette? She chewed a box open, and I saw what was inside. So I tackled Cuffy, and after we went a few rounds, he told me. He wasn't using. Not then. I wanted out, right then, like I said. For both of us. But by then Estrada knew about Amalie. And then Cuffy started using. And then you came. And I was afraid."

Not for himself. For me. And for Gran'Amalie.

I gathered up my purse and shawl, my eyes wet. "Come on," I whispered. "Let's go home."

"The long way, I hope." The twinkle was back in Mark's eyes.

We walked out of the smoke-filled jazz club into the Savannah night. The moon was shining, silvering the sea. The *Silver Cat* beckoned. So did Bonne Espérance, an hour's ride away. Home.

Whatever happened to Mark when the drug case came to court wasn't going to change one thing. Mark and I had only met this summer. Only weeks ago. But in those weeks we'd seen more of the truth about each other, more of what we each were made of, more of caring and sacrifice and endurance than a lot of couples saw in half a lifetime. We were bonded, and we both knew it.

The *Silver Cat* purred contentedly as we took the long way home back to Bonne Espérance.

ABOUT THE AUTHOR

NORMA JOHNSTON is the author of over eighty books for adults and young adults, including the *Carlisle Chronicles* series for Bantam Starfire and the acclaimed *Keeping Days* series. Ms. Johnston has traveled extensively around the world, and at various times has been a teacher, actress, play director, boutique owner, and free-lance editor. She is currently at work on a middle-grade horse story to be published as a Bantam Skylark book.